NO GIRLS allowed

Inspired by the True Story
of a Girl Who Fought for her
Right to Play

NATALIE CORBETT SAMPSON

NIMBUS
PUBLISHING
— NIMBUS.CA —

Copyright © 2019, Natalie Corbett Sampson

Nimbus Publishing Limited
3660 Strawberry Hill St, Halifax, NS, B3K 5A9
(902) 455-4286 nimbus.ca

Printed and bound in Canada
NB1429

This story is a work of fiction, inspired by a true story. Names, characters, incidents, and places, including organizations and institutions, either are the product of the author's imagination or are used fictitiously.

Cover and interior design: Heather Bryan
Editor: Penelope Jackson | Editor for the press: Emily MacKinnon

Library and Archives Canada Cataloguing in Publication

Title: No girls allowed : inspired by the true story of a girl who fought for her right to play / Natalie Corbett Sampson.
Names: Sampson, Natalie Corbett, 1976- author.
Identifiers: Canadiana 2019016056X | ISBN 9781771087773 (softcover)
Subjects: LCSH: Forbes, Tena—Childhood and youth—Juvenile fiction.
Classification: LCC PS8637.A53854 N62 2019 | DDC jC813/.6 —dc23

Nimbus Publishing acknowledges the financial support for its publishing activities from the Government of Canada, the Canada Council for the Arts, and from the Province of Nova Scotia. We are pleased to work in partnership with the Province of Nova Scotia to develop and promote our creative industries for the benefit of all Nova Scotians.

This novel is written with much appreciation to Tena Forbes for her generosity of time and sharing her story now, and for her bravery and perseverance then. Because of her efforts, and those of her peers, my own girls, Paxten and AnnaWen, can thrive on the ice.

Contents

CHAPTER 1

Last Skate
(August 1977)

"TINA! ARE YOU PACKING?" MOM CALLS from downstairs.

"Yes!" I say, even though I'm not. I toss my tennis ball against the wall again and catch it when it bounces back. My next toss hits too low, and the ball bounces off the wall into an empty box on the floor. There are boxes everywhere: on my dresser, on my bed, on my desk, on the floor. They're all open and half empty. Mom took a black marker and wrote labels on the side so I'd know what to put in each one: clothes, books, toys, stuffed animals. The tennis ball landed in one that says "shoes and boots." Why do I need a whole box for those? I have no idea. I only have, like, two pairs of sneakers. And my skates, I guess. I put them in there too, since Mom didn't label any boxes "sports equipment."

Inside the box the tennis ball is wedged under my white figure skate. I lift the skate out. Heavy, the white leather is creased and lined around the ankle, and the blade flashes the light from the ceiling into my eyes.

I hear a knock on the open door and turn around. "Tina, are you packing?" Mom asks again.

"Yes, see?" I say, putting the skate back into the box.

Mom smiles, but she's not fooled. She holds out her hand and says, "I'll pack the tennis ball with our summer things."

Busted.

I hand her the ball and flop back on the bed, arms crossed. Packing sucks. "Come on now, Tina, if you just focus you'll get it done and then you can go outside with J. R." She rests her hand on my head for a moment and I sigh. Kids outside are yelling, their sticks whacking against the pavement. I was heading out with my own stick and hockey gloves when Mom stopped me in the kitchen and asked if my boxes were full yet. Sucks!

I don't care much that we're moving; we've moved lots of times before. Dad says because he's a lawyer for the government they get to move him wherever they need him. And now they need him in Yarmouth.

I had to look on the map. It's right at the most southern tip of Nova Scotia.

Our new place looks cool, I just hate the whole packing part. We went up before school to visit with Dad and see the house he found. I even got to pick out my room. The window looks out over a field with a pond in the middle. If it's big enough for pond hockey, it'll be great.

But I finally turned ten this year, so I get to play real hockey too. In the rink. On a team. With painted lines and fans and a scoreboard to count all my goals. I can't wait. Real hockey, with real refs, not kids who just make up rules that help them win. Last year I wrote my Christmas list in September. The only thing on it was hockey skates. I told Mom and Dad, "If I can get hockey skates, it'll be the best Christmas ever." Everyone knows you can't play real hockey in figure skates.

Mom walks by my door again and says, "Come on, Tina! Stop daydreaming and get moving!" I was thinking of gliding over real painted lines.

"I am!" I call after her and go to the dresser. Now that I'm ten, I'm tall enough to see my reflection in the mirror above the dresser. My hair is messy. Even though I keep it shorter, I've got curls going everywhere. I smooth it down over my head and pull it back—it's almost long enough to put in a ponytail. Maybe I should grow it just a bit longer so I can tie it back? Or maybe I should just cut it shorter. In the meantime, I'd better get packing. I start with the top drawer, lifting my underwear and pyjamas into the box that says "clothes." One good thing about wearing mostly sweatpants and T-shirts is they roll up tight for packing. I make sure my Star Wars T-shirts are on top so I can find them easier when I unpack.

THE PHONE RINGS JUST SECONDS after we sit down for supper. "I'll get it!" I yell and beat J. R. to the yellow phone on the wall. He punches me in the arm, but Mom doesn't see it. She never sees it when he hits me. I pick up and say hello, twisting the spiral cord around the fingers of my left hand.

"Hello, Tina Marie, how was your day?" booms the voice on the other end. It's like Yarmouth is a street we could bike to instead of a town half a country away.

"Hi, Dad," I say, smiling. "It was fine. Did you register us yet?" He knows I'm talking about hockey, I ask him that every time he calls.

He laughs and says, "Not yet; the registration isn't open. You'll be the first to know when I do, okay? Maybe it won't open until after you're here, and you can come with me. Would you like that?"

"That would be far out!" I say, and it sounds like he might be laughing. Winter seems like forever away.

"Is your mother there? I have a few things I need to talk to her about."

"Yeah, hold on," I say and hold the receiver out toward Mom. "Dad wants to talk to you."

Mom stands up and walks across the kitchen to take the phone from me. "Thanks, honey. Now go eat up." She puts the phone to her ear and walks into the dining room. The spiral cord follows her, and I can see it jiggling a bit as she talks.

I cut a piece of chicken and plop it in my mouth. J. R.'s sitting across from me and Mom can't see me from the other room, so I kick him under the table. I can be sneaky too.

"What was that for?" he says, potatoes in his mouth.

"Nothing." I shrug. "How many days?"

J. R. rolls his eyes and shakes his head. His dark hair is floppy and bounces around. "One less than what I told you when you asked me last night. What's the big deal, anyway? We're moving to some crappy little town. You'll be sorry when we get there and there's nothing to do." He thinks he's so cool just because he's almost thirteen. Too cool for a small town in Nova Scotia, too cool for me. Too cool for anything.

"What do you mean, nothing to do? There's just as much there to do as here. I mean, there are kids there, so they have to have kid stuff to do."

J. R. makes a face that says he isn't so sure about that. He doesn't want to move. He got really mad when Dad told us he was being transferred again. He even shouted, then ran off to his room and slammed the door. Later I heard him telling Mom and Dad that he didn't want to leave his friends. I don't care so much. I mean, my friends are all right, but all you need to do to make friends is play sports. Join a team and there's a bunch of them ready to meet. Go outside with a ball and a hockey stick or a tennis racket and kids show up. That's been true wherever we've lived; here in Toronto or before, when we were in Winnipeg.

Mom comes back into the kitchen and hangs up the phone. "Your dad said hello, J. R. He also said the renovations on the house are coming along nicely and it should be ready for us when we move out there. Isn't that great?" I nod, but J. R. just shrugs, staring at his peas. "Finish up, kids. I have to meet someone at the rink. If you hurry, you can come with me and bring your skates."

She doesn't have to tell me twice. I stuff some potato in my mouth, then say, "Oh, but my skates are packed!"

"Do you remember which box?" Mom says. I nod. "Well then, you can get them back out. I'm afraid that'll be how we get along for the next few days."

AT THE RINK, I SIT on the team bench to tie my skates. I pull hard on the top of the laces to tighten the boot. It took a while to break them in but now my hockey skates fit perfectly, hugging my foot and ankle. I wrap the laces around the top of each boot and double knot them.

Mom's the head coach. She's meeting with one of her figure skaters on the visitors' bench while other skaters practice. I step on the ice, starting off slowly in a wide circle along the boards. I've done lots of lessons, but my favourite ice time is when I can do whatever I want. Even though it's a figure-skating practice, I'm wearing my hockey skates and working on all the moves I've seen René Robert do when the Sabres play on Hockey Night in Canada. Backward skating is my favourite. With two side pushes and a C-cut, I can be flying. And since we're on real ice, not a pond, I use the painted lines to know just where I am all the time. Usually I have to stick to one end, to stay out of the way of Mom's students, but while she's talking to some of them on the bench I can skate all the way around the ice. Flying. Maybe this is what a bird feels like.

By the time Mom calls me off the ice, my hair is wet against my neck. I practiced forward and backward, edges and circles and dekes. I know I have to work hard to get ready for the new season.

"Did you have fun?" Mom asks while we sit side by side and untie our skates.

"Yeah," I say. "I go a lot faster in these." I lift up my hockey skate. "The toe picks on figure skates get in the way."

Mom smiles but doesn't say anything. She used to

try and convince me that figure skating was better than hockey, and that I should stick with lessons to get better at jumps and tricks. She loves figure skating, so I guess she doesn't get why I don't love it too. I mean I do, but not as much as hockey. When I play hockey on the pond with the other kids? That's way more fun than doing twirls by myself. And if pond hockey is that fun, imagine how awesome it'll be to be on a real team with plays and passing!

Mom stands up, her boots on and her skates tucked away in her bag. "Take a good look, Tina; I think this is the last time we'll be here. I'll be busy getting everything ready for the move until your dad comes home, and he only has a few days to drive back to Nova Scotia. I don't think we'll have time to skate again."

I look up at the ice, the boards painted with advertising for local hardware stores and plumbers, the red and blue lines painted underneath the blade-scratched surface, the lights suspended from the frame and the dark scoreboard. Leaving is sad, but new places are exciting. Changes are always a bit of both.

CHAPTER 2

New House, New Net
(August 1977)

THE DRIVE FROM ONTARIO TO NOVA SCOTIA is super long. I bug J. R. until he finally agrees to play cards in the backseat if I'll leave him alone. But he only plays one game and then quits. Then I try finding letters of the alphabet on signs and licence plates along the highway. The worst part of the game is when I'm stuck on Z and I just have to keep looking for a Zellers. When I get bored I bug J. R. again and we bicker until Mom or Dad turns around and tells us to knock it off. I read almost all of my new *Star Wars* novel. I try to draw pictures of the Flintstones, but they never turn out right. Sometimes I just stare out the window at Ontario farms changing to hills, and the St. Lawrence River running beside the highway. Highway signs start showing French names that I try to say. I only talk louder when J. R. tells me to shut up.

I'M WISHING I HAD eaten all my lunch on the second day and wondering how long until supper when Dad says, "Look! Here we are!" I poke my head out the window to see flags lining the highway. Half are yellow with blue and red details, a big ship with open sails in the middle. Half are white with a blue X, a yellow and red shield in the middle where the lines meet. I remember when I studied the provincial flags in school I thought the New Brunswick one was kind of scary, with a lion in the sky attacking the ship. The Nova Scotia flag is pretty, the white and blue. The wind blows my bangs into my eyes. I push my hair out of my face and lick my lips and taste salt.

Later, Dad wakes me up, saying, "Tina, Tina, you'll want to see this. We're almost there." I push myself up and look out the window. The sun is coming down, but it's still light out. The car is moving slowly, and houses with large lawns and big trees slip by my window. The road ends, and Dad has to turn left or right. His blinker ticks as he turns right and then picks up speed again, passing a few shops and houses.

"Look there, kids, see that building up on the hill?" Out of the driver's side, at the top of a mowed lawn, is a short, wide building with lights already lit.

"What is it?" J. R. asks, blocking his window so I can't see. I scoot over behind Dad so I can look out better.

"That's the rink," Dad says, and I feel a buzz in my middle and a smile stretch across my face. The rink.

A few moments later, Dad steers the car gently off the road into a driveway. We bump and bounce over the uneven dirt path. Ahead our new house is lit up like it's alive and saying, "Welcome home!" The minute the car parks I shove my door open and hit the ground running, but I stop short as I round the car and face the garage.

At the side of the house is a hockey net! Its red frame flashes in the light from the porch and the soft netting falls around it. We had to leave our old rickety net at home. The Sturges up the road gave it to us. It was falling apart when we got it and Dad had to fix it with duct tape, but it was still good enough to shoot on. Mom said it wasn't worth transporting all the way to Yarmouth. I tried not to argue, but when she put it on the garbage pile for the movers, I had to look away so I didn't cry.

"What?" I shout. I can't help it. "Is it ours?"

"Of course it's ours, spaz; why else would it be in our driveway?" J. R. says, shoving me in the shoulder as he passes me, running to the net.

I follow and run my fingers along the bumps the rope made on the crossbar. "Look, it has pockets!" I say, pulling on the net hanging from the corner. I'm learning how to lift the puck, and I can already get it off the ground sometimes. As I poke my fingers through the pocket netting, I imagine hitting the target with the puck, shot after shot after shot. Soon I'll be able to do that.

"Well, we thought you'd like to practice before the season starts," Dad says, and we turn to look at him. He's standing beside Mom, his arm stretched around her shoulders. He's a bit taller than Mom and has J. R.'s floppy hair. Mom has my blond hair. Usually Dad's hair is tidy, but after our two-day drive it's all messed up. "Being from away and all, you'll both have to go in and show them you can play."

He laughs, but it still makes a pit of worry turn in my stomach. I'm so excited to play hockey, I never thought I might not be good enough. What if kids here are way better than in Toronto? I was one of the fastest skaters there, but maybe here I'm not good enough to play on a real team. I'll have to be sure to practice a lot before then.

"Come on now, kids, grab your bags. Let's get inside and start unpacking," Mom says, so I don't have time to worry.

I go back to the car, pull my bag off the back seat and over my shoulder, and turn to face the house. I stop to look at the lit-up windows, my parents opening the door with the light spilling out onto the porch, the red-framed net standing beside the house. Waiting. I smile and follow my family inside.

CHAPTER 3

First Day of School
(September 1977)

IT'S LUCKY I PACKED MY STAR WARS T-SHIRTS right where I could find them, because that's what I want to wear to school the first day. I usually don't care about clothes, but I want the other kids to know that we had cool stuff in Toronto too. I get dressed and jump down the stairs, skipping every other one.

"Tina, be careful!" Mom yells from the kitchen, but I'm already at the bottom. I walk into the kitchen and sit in my chair. Mom already has the bowls and the cereal boxes on the table. "Good morning," she says as I pour Life into my bowl. "Are you ready?"

"Yup," I say. My voice sounds more sure than my belly feels. I've gone to new schools lots of times; I should be used to this by now. But I still feel kind of icky and nervous. I try not to let on, though. That's one of the secrets: don't let anyone know you're scared.

J. R. comes into the kitchen behind my chair and messes up my hair with his big fat hand. "Jerk!" I say before I can stop myself.

"Tina, we don't call names," Mom says. She's pouring her coffee at the counter and doesn't see him mess my hair up. It's almost impossible to make my hair tidy. I brushed it forever upstairs and now I'm going to have to do it again. I glare at J. R., but he just smiles at me when he sits down in his chair across the table.

"Cereal," he grunts. I ignore him, so he stands up to reach across the table and grabs it himself.

"J. R. are you ready for your first day?" Mom asks. She brings her coffee to the table and sits down between us.

"Nothing to be ready for," J. R. says and then shovels cereal and milk into his mouth. "This town is dullsville." When he says that some milk dribbles down his chin and he wipes it with the back of his hand.

"That is not a great attitude to have," Mom says. J. R. doesn't say anything. Even he knows not to talk back to Mom. She keeps going though, talking to J. R. about attitude and appreciating different places. I don't bother to listen.

When I'm done my cereal I brush my teeth. By the door I put on my shoes and pick up my backpack. "Bye, Mom!" I yell into the kitchen.

Mom comes to the kitchen doorway. "Wait for your brother," she says.

"I know the way!" I say. I am not a baby who needs her big brother to walk her to school! I don't need that to be everyone's first impression of me when I walk into the schoolyard.

But Mom just says "Wait for your brother" again to let me know there's no point in arguing and she's not going to change her mind.

So I wait. It takes him a million years to brush his teeth and put on his shoes and he forgets two things in his room and has to go back up to get each one. By the time we're headed out the door I'm sure we're going to be late. Being late for your first day sucks.

"Remember, go to the office, they'll show you where to go!" Mom yells after us as we walk down the driveway. J. R. ignores her, but I turn around and wave to let her know I heard her. "Have a good day!" she adds.

We walk down the driveway to the street. I'm almost running to keep up with J. R.'s long steps, but I'm not going to admit that to him. I just concentrate on keeping up. When we get to the road, J. R. turns to me and says, "See ya, sucker!" and takes off running. There's no way I could keep up with him. If we were the same size, I bet I could beat him in a race, but his legs are way longer than mine.

"Jerk!" I yell after him. He doesn't stop and I don't really care. The school is down this road, turn left and then right, and down the next road. Super easy. I still walk fast, though. It's a good thing I do, too, because when I get to the school the bell goes off. I stop for a second right on the edge of the yard. Lots of kids are running from all over to line up at the doors on the side of the building. I wonder which ones are in grade four. There are kids smaller than me and kids bigger than me but one line has kids that are mostly my size. I bet that's them.

I watch them walk into the school then run to the front door where the office should be so I'm not late for class. When I go into the office J. R. is waiting in a chair. He's not sitting, he's leaned back like he needs a nap. Mom would tell him to sit up properly. The lady behind the desk says, "You must be Tina," and I look at her instead.

"Yes," I say. "Tina Marie Forbes." I hear J. R. sniff a laugh, but the lady and I both ignore him. Maybe she has an older brother too?

"Nice to meet you, Tina. I'm Miss Carlton, the secretary. You're in Mrs. Boudreau's class. I'll show you and Robert where your classrooms are and introduce you to your teachers."

J. R. grumbles, "J. R." He hates correcting everyone about his name, but that's no excuse for being rude.

"Yes, J. R. I'm sorry, I'll learn it eventually," Miss Carlton says and her voice kind of laughs. I like her already.

The school is way smaller than the one we went to in Toronto, so my classroom is easy to find. It's just down the hall and around one corner from the office. The door is open and the kids inside are yelling and talking and walking around. I'm glad class hasn't started yet—that means I'm not late. A teacher is sitting behind the desk, but when she looks up and sees us standing in the doorway, she stands and comes over. Miss Carlton talks first: "Mrs. Boudreau, this is Tina Forbes."

Mrs. Boudreau smiles at me, but it's not a real smile. She just sort of pushes her lips together. They don't go up into her cheeks and her eyes stay kind of angry. "Good morning, Tina. We've been waiting to meet you," she says. Her voice does not laugh like Miss. Carlton's.

I wish I could go with them when Miss Carlton says, "Have a great first day, Tina!" and "Come on, Rob—J. R., your class is just down this way." I'm stuck in the doorway. I should go in the classroom, but my feet don't move and my knees are wobbly. The Life cereal in my stomach is doing backflips, like in the commercial when the cereal jumps into the pool of milk.

"Tina, you can sit there, beside Shari," Mrs. Boudreau says. I look at the desks. Some kids are sitting in chairs, some are sitting on desks, some are standing in a group. I have no idea who Shari is or where she sits. My heart starts to beat faster and harder, but then a girl sitting beside an empty chair waves and smiles at me. She must be Shari.

I try not to stare right at her when I walk toward her, but I like to figure out a bit about people when I meet them by the way they look. Mom always says "You can't judge a book by its cover," but there are some things you can tell just by looking. Shari's black hair is fancy, with half of it pulled back in a ponytail and the rest long. She's looking in a red purse with white polka dots and a big red button on the front. I don't know anyone my age who carries a purse. But she's wearing gym shorts and a T-shirt. Hopefully that means she likes to do fun stuff at recess, like play Red Rover or soccer baseball. You can't do those things in a dress, so if she was wearing a dress maybe she wouldn't like them—but she's not. Her T-shirt has a picture of Jaime Sommers on it. I like to watch *The Bionic Woman* too.

"Hi," I say when I get to the desk. I put my book bag under the desk and sit down.

"Hi, I'm Shari," she says. She puts her hand out for me to shake like we're grown-ups. I shake it.

"I'm Tina," I say.

"Where are you from?" Shari asks. That's always the first question.

"Toronto," I say. She looks a bit confused so I add, "That's in Ontario."

"Yeah, I know!" she says, but she sounds excited, not like she's mad at me for thinking she didn't know where Toronto was. "My aunt lives there. I went to visit her like two years ago? We went up in the CN Tower. Have you been up there? You can see everything up there. I asked Aunt Cathy if we could see Yarmouth from there, but she didn't think so. Probably close, though."

I only have time to nod and smile while Shari talks before Mrs. Boudreau is at the front of the class clapping her hands and asking us to all be quiet and sit down. I'm pretty sure Shari and I are going to be friends. It's a pretty good first day if you meet a friend right away.

CHAPTER 4

Registration
(September 1977)

"TINA, YOU NEED TO HURRY UP IF YOU WANT to come with me," Dad calls up the stairs.

"I'm coming!" I yell back. I stuff all the clothes I'm supposed to be carefully putting away into the bottom drawer and lean against it to push it closed. I'll sort them later. Maybe.

I race into the hall and down the stairs two at a time. Mom calls from the kitchen, "Slow down on the stairs!" but I'm already at the bottom, shoving my feet into my dirty white sneakers.

"Ready!" I announce while I step toward the door.

"Tie your shoes," Dad says.

I don't want to, but I don't dare argue. Not today.

Not on the way to hockey registration. I've been waiting for this way too long to miss going with him. "Is J. R. coming?" I ask while I tie the second shoe.

"Nope," he says, waiting, his hand on the doorknob while my fingers twist the laces into lopsided knots and bows.

"How come?" Why wouldn't he want to go?

"We're just filling out the registration papers, Tina," Dad says, as if it's nothing that I'm signing up to play hockey. Today. Finally.

"I know!" I say, bouncing up from tying my shoes. He smiles. He pushes the door open and I follow him to the car.

The day is warm for the end of September, so I crank my window down the minute the door closes. It feels like summer, sunny and warm. Dad backs out of our driveway and I lean my shoulders out of the window to feel the air on my face.

I know some people say they don't like winter, but I don't get it. Winter is playing in the snow and sledding and skating, and this year, for me? Hockey. Finally, I'm old enough to be on a real team. While the houses pass by, I wonder what colour my jersey might be. Red like the Canadiens? Hopefully blue like the Sabres!

"Tina, sit down in your seat." Dad always says that, and I still always forget. I sit back and look up at him. He smiles at me. "Excited?"

"Yeah," I say, nodding. "Do you think I'll get to play centre?"

"I think it'll depend who else is on your team." He glances at me just long enough for me to see his face is serious; not quite a frown, but his smile is gone. "Remember, Tina, there are kids who have played here for a while. You're new to this league and this town. You'll have to earn a chance to play centre by working hard."

"I'm a good skater," I say, even though I know he's right.

"You are, that's for sure," Dad says, but it sounds like he's not saying everything he's thinking. He turns the car into the parking lot of the Scotiabank building, marked by the large red "S" over the door.

"Why are we here?" I ask.

When Dad says, "This is where the registration is," I remember him telling Mom that registration wasn't at the rink. Seems weird, but a lot of things grown-ups do seem weird. "Ready?" His smile returns when I nod. "Let's go."

Dad takes my hand while we cross the parking lot. I'm too old for that, but like with tying my shoes, I don't want to argue right now. I'm too excited. Dad holds the door open for me and I walk in ahead of him. It's just a regular, boring bank, even if the hockey registration is happening here. The tellers are behind a tall desk and people are lined up on a long rug between two round, soft tubes. Regular bank stuff.

I sigh and my shoulders hang a bit. I guess I hoped there would be a registration table with other kids signing up and coaches asking all the players how they can skate. I even practiced in the mirror in the bathroom, saying, "I'm all right," so they know I'm a good skater but not a bragger.

Dad goes to the information desk and I hear him say he's there to register. He's not. I am! The lady smiles and asks him to wait a minute, then disappears down the hall.

When she returns a minute later a tall man in a suit is following her. His tie is blue with small white dots and it's crooked at the top, the knot pulled to one side so that the long part of the tie is hanging down on one side of the buttons on his shirt. The buttons around his belly are kind of stretched so that there are gaps between them. He walks right to Dad with his hand outstretched.

"Hi, I'm Pete Hickman, registrar for Yarmouth Minor Hockey," he says. His voice is low and booming, like he's laughing.

"Rob Forbes. How are you?" Dad says, shaking his hand and smiling at him. Suddenly I feel kind of strange standing in the middle of the bank where everyone can see me. I take a step closer to Dad. When Dad lets go of Mr. Hickman's hand, he puts it behind my back.

"Great, great! You're here for hockey registration?"

"Yes!" I say. I can't help it.

Mr. Hickman smiles at me and then says to Dad, "I have the registration forms in my office. Come with me." He turns away from us and starts back the way he'd come. Dad follows him and I stick close.

In his office there's a desk and a chair behind it, with two chairs in front of it. A black phone is on the desk, the number dial in the middle shiny and clear. He has notebooks and papers neatly stacked in one corner, and a blotter with doodles covers the middle. He sits in the single chair and Dad sits across the desk from him. I want to sit on Dad's lap but take a seat in the chair beside him instead, because I'm old enough to play hockey and that's too old to sit on Dad's lap at registration.

"I have them here somewhere," Mr. Hickman says. I don't know how, but he's looking through the pile of papers on his desk without even messing it up. "Ah here, how many do you need?" His hands stop moving and he looks up at Dad with a big smile on his face.

"Two please," Dad says, and he looks at me. I smile back. My cheeks feel hot and bunched up because I'm smiling so much.

"Right, here you go." Mr. Hickman pushes the pages across the table to Dad and hands him a pen. "We're anticipating a great season this year. We've had our numbers increase every year recently. The boys are having such a great time playing."

I stop listening to Mr. Hickman while I watch Dad's square handwriting appear behind his pen as he carefully fills out the first line with T-I-N-A. He stops writing, so I look up at his face and see him smiling at me. He winks, then starts writing again and finishes the form. He pulls the blank page out from under it and starts again with J. R.'s name and birthdate. He lays the pen down on top of the pages and pushes them back across the blotter to Mr. Hickman.

"And how much should I make the cheque out for?" Dad asks him, pulling a folded cheque from his wallet.

"Well, it's eighteen dollars a boy, but we have a family discount, so that it's a total of thirty dollars for two," Mr. Hickman says as he reads over J. R.'s form. "Excellent, excellent. We're happy to have Robert join us."

"J. R.," I say, and then my ears burn hot.

"I'm sorry?" Mr. Hickman says to me, then looks at Dad. I want to explain, but nothing comes out when I open my mouth.

Dad laughs a little. "We call Robert 'J. R.' His mother doesn't like 'junior' and two 'Roberts' is one too many."

"I see, of course. J. R. We'll be happy to have J. R. Our peewee team is a great group of boys." Mr. Hickman switches the bottom page—mine—to the top. "And who do we have here?" His eyes move back and forth over the top of the page, then look up at Dad, and then back to the page. "This name, 'Tina,' is that a...girl?"

Dad smiles at him and puts his hand out to rest on my shoulder. "Yes, Tina, my daughter here. She's very excited to play. It's been tough for her to wait until she's old enough."

Mr. Hickman looks at me, but it takes a moment before he smiles. His smile looks kind of like when J. R. is waiting for Mom to put rubbing alcohol on a scraped knee and he is trying to be brave. "I'm afraid we don't have enough girls for a girls' team. We tried a couple of years ago and only had six girls sign up. I'm sorry to say the interest is just not there." He says all that to Dad. He's not looking at me anymore.

"That's okay," Dad says and squeezes my shoulder. "She's happy to play wherever she's placed. She just wants to play."

"Yes, well, I'm afraid we don't register girls to play on the boys' teams."

What?

When they stop talking I can hear the clock on the wall *tick, tick, ticking*. I hear someone walk past the closed door, a voice but no words, and more clicking of high-heeled shoes. I can hear my heart, too. It's beating hard and almost in sync with the ticking of the clock. What does he mean, they don't register girls?

"I'm sorry?" Dad says.

"We don't allow girls to play with boys."

I blink fast so my eyes can't fill up with tears. I'm too old to cry. Too old to cry. Do not cry!

Tick, tick, tick goes the clock. *Boom, swish, boom, swish* goes my heart in my ears. My throat hurts and I'm holding my teeth tight. I'm not smiling anymore, but my cheeks are prickling. What does he mean?

Dad clears his throat and takes his hand off my shoulder. He puts both of his hands on the desk, pushing his palms against the blotter, his long fingers spread out. "I don't quite understand, Mr. Hickman, why you would not allow my daughter to play. She's a good skater. Her mother is a figure-skating coach. Tina has been on skates since she could walk. She's played hockey on the pond with kids for years, so she understands the game and is capable with a stick and puck. She just wants to play on a team—"

Mr. Hickman holds his hand up and Dad stops talking. Dad folds his hands together so tight the knuckles are white. He does that when he's getting angry, because he doesn't yell like some people do when they're mad. Mr. Hickman's smile is gone, and his mouth and eyes have an angry frown. An up-and-down line between his eyebrows is showing. I want to leave. This office is too small for three of us if Mr. Hickman and Dad are both angry. But he won't take my registration paper. I'm not registered yet.

"We follow the rules of the Nova Scotia Minor Hockey Council, Mr. Forbes, and the rules are quite clear that hockey is a sport for boys," Mr. Hickman says. He doesn't sound like he's laughing anymore. His voice is low, like a big dog's growl. Dad leans back and Mr. Hickman stands up from his desk. "I'd be happy to help you initiate a girls' league. As I said, we did have six girls interested a couple of years ago. I suspect those girls are older now, and perhaps their interest has waned, but if Tina were to talk to some of her little friends, perhaps she could convince a few to come out and try it."

Tick, tick, tick goes the clock. Then my father stands up. I stand up too, but my knees feel really shaky. I'm not really sure what is going on—what does he mean, I can't play? I am ten, after all; that's the age that real teams start. I don't care if there are other girls or not. I'm used to playing with boys. Mr. Hickman hands one paper back to Dad, the one with my name at the top, and says, "I hope this will be the end of this matter."

Dad waits three clock ticks, then takes the paper and folds it neatly in half. When he does things slowly and carefully I know he's really mad. "I see," Dad says. "I'll be in touch." Mr. Hickman holds his hand out, but Dad doesn't see it. Instead he smiles at me and puts his hand back on my shoulder. "Let's go, Tina," he says while turning me toward the door.

He's still holding my registration, though, and I don't want to leave until I'm registered to play, even if this office is too small and Dad and Mr. Hickman are angry.

"But Dad—"

"It's all right, Tina. We'll sort this all out," he says. His hand stays on my shoulder as we walk out of the room and leave the bank. It keeps me moving forward, even though I want to go back in the small office and make Mr. Hickman take my registration paper.

In the car I don't roll down the window. I sit cross-legged, watching my hands twist around each other, fingers tangled up. I want to ask Dad why he kept my paper, but I don't really want to hear his answer. I'm scared I know why—maybe I really can't play. But I don't get it.

Dad doesn't say anything as he backs the car out of the parking spot and heads through the lot, but his knuckles are still white when he holds the steering wheel. When we're driving away from the bank, he says, "We'll figure it out, Tina," and that makes all the words bubbling in my head come out.

"I can't play because I'm a girl? Is that what he said? What difference does that make? I'm ten. Before they said I had to be ten and I waited and now I'm ten and I want to play. I can skate. You told them I can skate, so why can't I play?" At the end of my words, my voice does that wobbly thing and I'm worried I might cry. That won't solve anything. I press my mouth shut and stare out the window. I'm not going to cry. I'm not going to cry. But the houses and trees are blurry, and one drop falls from my right eye. Just one though. I swipe it off my face.

"I know, Tina. You're a very good skater. I'll talk to them and work this out. I think maybe Mr. Hickman doesn't know the rules, and we just have to talk to someone else." Dad takes one hand off the wheel and squeezes my knee. I don't look at him, because I don't want him to know I was crying. I take a deep breath and feel a little bit better. I take another. Dad knows how to solve problems. He'll fix it.

CHAPTER 5

Weekend Recap
(September 1977)

WHEN I SIT IN MY DESK AT SCHOOL ON Monday, Chris Murray walks past staring at me and grinning. I haven't talked to him much, I don't really know him. Sometimes we are on the same soccer team at recess, but it's not like we talk at all then. He stops and puts his hands on my desk, leaning closer on his palms.

"Hey, Tony, how was your weekend?"

I open my mouth and then close it again because I can't think of what to say. His voice is so mean, and why did he call me Tony? My ears burn and my eyes feel prickly.

"Hey!" Shari says, and I turn to see her walk up

to her desk beside mine and put her purse down. I smile at her, and when I turn back Chris is gone, walking down the aisle to his desk near the back. I'm glad he's gone and I didn't have to come up with something to say to him.

Mrs. Boudreau is clapping at the front of the class, the claps are sharp and loud above our chattering. "Take your seats!" she says. Over the intercom the principal tells us to stand up for the anthem, and all the chairs scrape on the floor as we all stand up at the same time. I try to stand still; I know it's important and respectful to stand still while "O Canada" plays, even if it's just on the intercom at school. But behind me I can hear Chris and Andy whispering and laughing. I turn my head just a bit to look back and Chris is looking right at me. I turn back around fast, but it's not fast enough. He laughs louder. "Christopher! Attention please!" Mrs. Boudreau snaps over the scratchy music, and the back of the classroom goes quiet.

After the anthem and the announcements, Mrs. Boudreau starts the class the same way she does every Monday: "Good morning, boys and girls. Did anyone have anything exciting happen on the weekend? Yes, Lindsay?"

Lindsay sits one row in front of me and two rows over. Her hand is usually up before Mrs. Boudreau finishes the question. "We got a new puppy!" she squeals.

"Well, puppies are quite a bit of work. What is his name?" Mrs. Boudreau says. She doesn't smile. How does someone not smile when they're talking about a puppy? Even I'm smiling, and I don't really like Lindsay all that much. She spends recess sitting on the steps by the grade-one door with a few other girls. They are always laughing and I don't get why, even when I can hear what they're saying. She wears a dress to school every day. Even when we have gym class.

"His name is Radar," Lindsay says. "After the guy in *M*A*S*H*." I'm not allowed to watch *M*A*S*H*. Mom and Dad say it's an adult show. I don't even know what makes it an adult show.

Mrs. Boudreau has moved on. "Yes, Christopher?" she asks. I turn in my seat to see him lower his hand. Chris doesn't usually put his hand up in class.

"I registered for hockey," Chris said. But he's not looking at Mrs. Boudreau when he says that; he's looking right at me with that weird, mean smirk still on his face. "I'm going to be on the Leafs. We'll probably win every game this year—all the boys on my team are really good." I'm sure I didn't imagine it that his voice went a little funny when he said "boys," and I don't like the way he's grinning at me now. I turn to the front and look at the "JEPA" carved on my desk. I run my finger along the grooves.

"Hockey is a very important sport in our country," Mrs. Boudreau says. "Rebecca? What do you have to share?"

I don't hear what Rebecca says, because I'm trying to figure out what is going on. First Chris stops at my desk and calls me "Tony," even though he knows my name. And then he put up his hand for maybe the first time all year just to tell the class he registered for hockey, but he was looking at me, and probably half of the other boys—Oooh. Probably half of the other boys registered too. But not the girls. And not me. So that's what this is all about: me trying to register for hockey and not being allowed because I'm a girl.

I don't know how everyone finds out everything in this town, but they do. Maybe Mr. Hickman from the bank knows Chris's dad, and he told him that a girl tried to register for hockey. I can just imagine them laughing and laughing about how silly it was. But it's not silly.

My ears have stopped burning, but now my heart is pounding fast. I bet Shari could hear it if she listened close enough. My eyes are more than prickly now, and I'm scared I'm going to cry. I curl my fingers up into fists and press my knuckles into my thighs under the desk. I concentrate on not crying. Think of something else—playing catch with Dad in the yard, eating Mom's strawberry shortcake, even what Lindsay's dumb dog might look like. When the feeling that I might cry is gone, I take a deep breath and turn to look back at Chris again. At first he's not looking at me but then he does. I make sure my eyes are squinty and my mouth is tight so I can give him the meanest glare I can come up with.

"Tina, eyes front, please; we're going to get started," Mrs. Boudreau says, and Chris points forward as if I didn't understand her words. I glare for just a second more before I turn to the front. "All right, class, we're going to start with math this morning. A pop quiz. Take out a blank piece of paper and put everything else away." The whole class groans but I don't care about a stupid math quiz. I have bigger problems to deal with.

CHAPTER 6

Rules
(October 1977)

I'M POKING MY FORK INTO THE PORK ROAST ON my plate. I've already stick-handled my peas away from the mashed potatoes. When I glance up at the clock again, Mom's looking at me with her I'm-watching-you frown. I spear a pea on each tine of the fork and put them in my mouth. It's been two weeks. Registration is over. Every day when Dad gets home, I ask if he knows anything else, but this afternoon Mom told me to "let him catch his breath" before I start asking him about hockey, so I decided to wait fifteen minutes after we sit down for dinner. I have four minutes to go. Dad's telling Mom some story. I'm not listening close enough to know what it is, but I hear the words "court" and "defendant" and "judge" and "bailiff," so I know it's about his work.

Two bites of pork and a mouthful of potatoes later, the fifteen minutes are up. When Dad stops telling his story to take a sip of his coffee, I jump in. "Dad? Did you hear anything about hockey?"

"Again with the hockey?" J. R. says. It sounds almost like a growl. I ignore him.

Dad puts his mug down and looks at Mom. I've seen that look. It means they know something I don't. But he's not smiling like it's good news. My hand hurts and I see I'm holding my fork so tight my skin is white. I put the fork down on my plate, careful not to clang it.

"Tina, I've spoken with Mr. Hickman and other members of the Association—they're the ones who run the hockey league and make the rules for registration."

I nod. I understand. Hurry up with the rest.

"They all say that it is indeed a rule that girls cannot play with boys."

My stomach feels icky and cold and the pork and potato in my mouth feel gross all of a sudden. I swallow.

"But that's not fair!" I say, but it only comes out as a whisper. I wipe a tear off my face before J. R. sees it and calls me a baby.

"I don't think so either," Dad says, and he tries to smile. "I am going to talk to the people who make their rules."

J. R. asks, "Who's that?" His mouth is full so it sounds like "hoowa."

"J. R., manners please," Mom says.

"Well, let's see. These gentlemen make the rules for the Yarmouth Minor Hockey Association. But that association answers to the Nova Scotia Minor Hockey Council, which looks at all of the province, and they get their rules from the Canadian Amateur Hockey Association."

I don't really care about all that stuff; I just want to play hockey. "So who made this rule?" I ask. "And who can change it?"

"That's exactly what I'm trying to find out. If I can find the source of the rule and demonstrate the discrimination that it entails...." Dad keeps talking for a bit longer, but I can't follow what he's saying.

"Discrimation?" I ask when he stops talking. "What's that?"

He smiles. "Dis-crim-in-a-tion," he says slowly. "That's what it's called when a person says you can't do or have something just because of who you are or what you look like. In this case, not letting you play hockey because you're not a boy is, I think, discrimination."

"Like Martin Luther King?" J. R. says. I look at him. His cheek is puffed out, full of food. He tosses his brown hair out of his eyes by flicking his head back quickly. He needs a haircut.

"Yes, son, that's similar. Martin Luther King Jr. led what was called the civil rights movement in the United States to stop discrimination against people who are Black. Here in Canada we had the case of Viola Desmond. Have either of you heard of her?" J. R. and I both shake our heads. "She lived in Halifax. She sat in a seat at the movie theatre that was supposed to be for white people only. When she refused to move, they arrested her. Like Dr. King, she stood up against discrimination."

"Or sat down, really," J. R. says and laughs. Dad gives him a stern look. I don't know what my brother's laughing at; discrimination is not funny.

"It's not fair," I say again.

"No, it wasn't, Tina," Dad says. "They charged Viola Desmond with an offence related to taxes, not race, but it helped start the civil rights movement here in Canada."

But I'm not talking about the woman in the theatre; I'm talking about me. It's not fair that I can't play hockey just because I'm a girl. I can skate, I can shoot, I can stickhandle as good as the boys. "So can I just play anyway? And go against their discrimination?"

Dad smiles at me. "Let's see what happens when I talk to the other people before we get ahead of ourselves, eh?"

"I just want to play hockey," I say. This time two tears sneak out and slip down my face before I can wipe them away. J. R. snickers.

Dad nods. "I know, honey."

"That's enough of that talk for tonight," Mom says. "Finish up your dinners and we'll play a game of Trouble before you get ready for bed."

J. R. rolls his eyes. I guess he's too cool for Trouble too.

CHAPTER 7

Soccer Field Battle
(November 1977)

THE WIND IS COLD, SO I FOLD MY SCARF around my face to cover my nose and mouth. I take my mitten off to knock on Shari's door, then rush to put it back on before my fingers freeze. She comes to the door a second later, swinging her *Charlie's Angels* backpack onto her back. "Bye, Mom!" she yells back into the house, and her mom yells back as I turn back to the sidewalk. Shari falls in beside me. "Brrr! It's cold!" she says.

"Yeah. I can't wait for it to snow," I say.

"Last year we had snowbanks up to here!" Shari says, holding her blue mitten up over her head. "We dug out the middle and made a fort. I wanted to sleep in it, but Mom said it was too cold."

"We used to live across the street from a school," I say. "In the winter, the field would flood and freeze so we could skate on it. We went there every day after school. It was far out!"

"I wish we had something like that. The salt water never freezes. There's nowhere to skate that we can walk to."

"There's the rink," I say. Mom has already started coaching kids there. If she doesn't have too many students she brings me along to skate. I stay down at one end while they're working and practice my crossovers and edges. "And I think the pond behind my house might be good for skating."

Shari scrunches up her nose. "It's an awfully small pond. More like a puddle." She's right, but I'm still hoping it's big enough to at least shoot on. It doesn't need to be very big for that.

We're almost to the school, so there are more kids on the sidewalks. Two boys race past Shari and me, and the one with a black leather jacket pushes between us. "Watch it!" I say when he pushes my shoulder and I stumble forward.

The boy turns and grins at me. It's a mean smile. He's bigger than me. I bet he's in J. R.'s grade, or maybe even older. "Whatcha gonna do about it,

Tony?" He tugs at the collar of his jacket to pull it upright. Who does he think he is, the Fonz? His friends laugh and they all take off running into the schoolyard.

Shari's looking at me. "Never mind him," I say before she can ask a question. "He's a chump."

But Shari asks anyway. "What was he talking about?"

I shrug and say, "I dunno."

But I do know. It's been happening more and more lately. Boys in school keep teasing me, calling me boy names, saying stuff about wanting to be a boy or acting like a boy. I just ignore it; what else can I do? I'm glad when the bell rings just as we get to the edge of the schoolyard and Shari and I have to run to line up with our class at the door. Maybe that's why people say "saved by the bell."

At recess I join in with the other kids playing soccer in the field. It's mostly boys, but Shari and I join in and so does a girl in grade five named Jennifer. After all the boys are picked, David picks me for his team and I join his side. The other captain picks Jennifer, so David picks Shari, and we get to be on the same team. We get the ball first and I race out to the right side of the field, trying to get open. David inbounds the ball and all of us move forward toward the net. I deke and turn, outrunning Chris, who is trying to stick to me. Finally I break open and call for the ball, and Mike kicks it up to me. I race toward the net, staring at the spot the keeper has left open by his left hand, but at the last minute I side kick it—without looking, which is the trick—over to David on the other side. The keeper can't move over quick enough and David kicks it past him. Goal for us! The other kids cheer and Shari grins at me, but there's not very much time to celebrate as the other team inbounds it and we work our way back to the other side of the field.

This time it's my job to stick to Chris, to make sure he doesn't get a chance to receive the ball. I watch him and try to stay between him and the ball as we all run closer and closer to the other net. At the last minute he dodges me and breaks toward the ball, and there's nothing I can do about the pass he gets right from Alan's foot to his. He turns toward the net and kicks the ball ahead of him, picking up speed. I run faster, cutting the distance between us with each stride. I'm small but fast. Maybe the fastest out here, except for David and maybe Mike. Faster than Chris for sure. We get to the ball at the same time and I slide feet-first and kick the ball away from him. He trips over my legs, falls to the ground, and rolls forward.

The ball rolls to a player from my team and he dribbles it up the field. I get up and jog after the ball and the other kids. Chris runs past, hitting my shoulder with his, and yells, "Watch it!" He turns and runs backward, glaring at me. "Why don't you

go play jump rope with the girls, where you belong?"
He glares at me once more as he trots up the field
after the rest of the group.

I know I should just ignore him and keep playing,
but I don't feel like it anymore. I stop running, then
stand and watch the kids kick the ball around the
other net. My eyes are stinging so I blink, blink,
blink to make them feel better. Shari sees me and
runs back to where I'm standing. "You okay?" she
asks.

"This is boring. Let's go do something else."

She looks at me a minute, her eyes squinting like
she's trying to figure out a problem. She doesn't
believe me, but she says, "Okay," and we walk back
toward the school.

Shari leads us to a small circle of girls from our
class, Lindsay and Sara and Robyn, who wave at
her when she gets close. Everyone likes Shari. The
girls are laughing about something when we walk up.
"Hey," Robyn says, stepping back to open the circle
so there's space for us to stand. I follow Shari into the
circle and smile, laugh a little too even though I don't
know what they're laughing about. I try to listen
to what they're saying—something that happened
on *The Waltons* last night—but I keep looking past
them to the boys playing soccer on the field.

CHAPTER 8

The Human Rights Act
(November 1977)

I FEEL THE BALL BOUNCING OFF THE STICK blade as I push and pull it back and forth, careful to keep my eyes up on the target of the net. Learning to stickhandle without looking at the puck is important. I count down five more taps, four, three, two, one, then shoot the ball at the net. It misses by a bit and bounces under the bushes. That makes three under there now. Time to find them. I set my stick against the net and crawl under the twigs. The ground is cold on my knees through my pants, and I'm glad

I have my hockey gloves on between my hands and the frozen grass.

"If you hit the net, you wouldn't have to waste time in the bushes," J. R. calls behind me as I grab the third ball.

"If you hit the net we'd have more than three balls," I shout back. When I run out of balls, I go find them. When J. R. runs out of them, he gives up and goes back inside.

I put two balls on the grass to the side of the driveway and go back to passing one back and forth with my stick. Ten, nine, eight, seven....

"I heard some of those guys at school," J. R. says from the porch. I look up but concentrate on keeping the ball moving side to side. He's leaning both elbows on the railing, tipping his head and shoulders over so that his feet swing up off the porch. If Dad saw him he'd tell him to cut it out, the porch railing is not a jungle gym. "It's your own fault, you know."

Ignore him. I shrug. I've lost count, so I look at the net and shoot. This time the ball scoots right between the red bars, bouncing off the back netting. "I don't care," I say. I kinda do, though. It sucks to be teased and called Tony and even meaner names, but there's not really anything I can do about it.

"Well, you might not care, but I do," J. R. says after a second. "They're pulling my chain too. Loser by association. You could just knock it off."

I'm pushing the second ball back and forth with my stick. "Knock what off?" I say, even though I know, and then shoot the ball. Hard. It bounces off the frame and comes back toward me. I shoot it as it rolls closer and it lands in the net.

"You know what I mean," J. R. says, then adds, "this whole hockey thing."

I want to say: "Easy for you to say, you get to play hockey just by signing up." But I don't because he wouldn't get it. He likes hockey, but he doesn't love it like I do. I stop playing with the ball and look up at him. "Soon the hockey people will change their minds and let me play and then everyone will forget about it."

"Fat chance," J. R. says.

My eyes tear up as I swing the ball with my slap shot and the ball goes blurry. I miss the hit, tapping just the top part of the ball so it bounce-rolls into the net. I rub my arm against my face and hope it looks like I'm wiping off sweat not tears. The last thing I need is J. R. seeing me cry.

A horn beeps on the road and I turn to see Dad pulling into the driveway. Just in time! He rolls toward the house slowly and then parks, while J. R. and I race to meet him as he gets out. "Why hello there! What a nice welcome home. How was school?"

J. R. looks at me for a second and I wonder if he wants to tell Dad what the other kids are saying, so

I glare at him and say, "Good!" before he can say anything at all. If Dad knew J. R. was being teased too, would he make me give up?

J. R. nods and looks back and Dad and says, "Good," too.

Dad puts his big hand on my head and messes my hair, then does the same to J. R. "Great, that's what I like to hear. Let's go in and see what's for supper." I want to ask him if he talked to anyone about the registration rules today. I want to ask if the Nova Scotia people or the Canada people have said they'll tell the Yarmouth people that's not the rule, but I remember what Mom said about letting him catch his breath, so I wait. It's not easy, but that seems to be all I can do.

I push the potatoes away from the green beans and eat them first, poking the four tines of the fork through each bean until the fork is full. I eat the pork chop, cutting a triangle off and popping it into my mouth before cutting the next one. When I'm done Mom asks me to clear the dishes while she cuts pieces of cherry pie for dessert.

Mom and Dad keep talking and I don't have a chance to ask anything without interrupting. Then J. R. lets his fork clatter onto his plate and asks, "Can I be excused?" He looks at Mom, then Dad, then back to Mom. I'm not finished my pie. I like to eat it slowly so it lasts longer, enjoying the way the tart cherries squish against the roof of my mouth.

Instead of answering him, our parents look at each other. Mom nods, but then Dad says, "In a minute. It's time for a chat."

This does not sound good.

He tries to smile, but his mouth just kind of pushes out. "As you know, I've spoken with many people about the rule. I've talked to the members of the Yarmouth Minor Hockey Association, and above them the Nova Scotia Minor Hockey Council, and above them the Canadian Amateur Hockey Association. It seems the folks here in Yarmouth are not willing to change this rule, and the other associations are supporting that decision."

"So Tina can't play," J. R. says. He doesn't sound disappointed. He sounds like he wants to add "I was right, na-na-na-boo-boo!"

"That is what they're saying," Dad says.

So that's it. Even though I'm old enough and good enough, I still can't play. I blink fast. I'm not going to cry. I clench my hands tight, poking my nails into my palms. I get the feeling that everyone is looking at me, but I stare at my half-eaten pie. The tart cherries feel like they're climbing out of my stomach into my throat.

"You still have skating, Tina. You can sign up for more figure-skating lessons so you can go to the rink more often. And we'll make a bigger effort to get out more often to play on the pond," Mom says.

"The pond is too small!" I yell. "It's not even a pond, it's a puddle!" My voice cracks on that last word so I stop. I stand up, my chair scraping against the floor loudly, and try to leave.

"Tina, sit down," Dad says in his serious, better-listen-the-first-time voice, so even though I want to run up to my room and slam my door, I slump back into my chair. "I know you're upset, but please lower your voice."

"It's not fair." I am not going to cry.

"No, it's not," Dad says. "There is another option." When he says that, I look up at him. I knew he could fix it. "Have you heard of the Human Rights Act?" I shake my head, and he looks at my brother. "Have you?" J. R. shrugs. "You remember we talked about discrimination?"

"Yeah, saying I can't play because I'm a girl is discrimination," I say.

"Yes, that's what I believe," he says. "Now the Human Rights Act was passed by the Canadian government this year. It's a law that makes it illegal to discriminate or stop someone from doing something because of their age or gender or the colour of their skin."

"So they can tell the hockey association that they have to let me play?"

Dad smiles at me, and Mom says, "It's not that simple, Tina."

"But if it's the law...."

"Your mother is right: it's not that simple. The Human Rights Act is the law, but we would have to prove that you have the right to play hockey, and that that law applies to this situation. It may involve lawyers and a judge and maybe even a court case."

"Okay," I say. I can do that. Maybe it'll work out after all!

"Tina, honey, you have to understand." Mom is talking to me but giving Dad a bit of a dirty look. "That would take time, first of all. And if we make a court case about playing, some people will be angry about it. There may be people who are unkind toward you at school and around town. You may be teased."

"Why should they be mad? It's the law!"

"Well, I'm sure there are people who think it's not the law. Maybe they feel the law does not say that girls can play hockey. Some people believe they have the right to say hockey is only for boys and that fighting against that is wrong." While Mom says this, she looks at me the way she does when she's trying to figure out what I'm thinking or if I'm telling the truth.

"Do you think that?" I mean to say it loudly, but it comes out as a whisper.

Mom looks over at Dad for a minute, then says, "No. I think you have the right to play." She smiles.

"Then how do we do it?" My voice is back.

"We would file a complaint with the Human Rights Commission—that's a group of people who have the job of listening to people who feel there is discrimination. They will listen to our story and decide if there is discrimination happening. From there we can take Yarmouth Minor Hockey before a judge, who will decide whether the rule is fair or if it should be changed."

"Okay. Let's do it."

Dad nods but looks around at Mom and J. R. before turning to me. "The reason we're talking like this as a family is that it's likely to affect all of us. I think we all need to agree that it's worth whatever consequence to try to take this forward." He looks at my brother. "J. R.? What do you think?"

J. R. shrugs, so I say quickly, "I'm already getting teased. Some guys call me 'Tony.' But I don't care. If they want to tease me, I can take it. I'll just ignore them." Easier said than done, but I will do it.

Dad smiles at me but looks back at J. R. "Son? What do you think?"

J. R. shrugs again. I hold my breath. If he tells them that he doesn't want me to because he gets teased too, will they decide it's not fair to him? That's not fair to me! He's staring at his pie plate, tracing the fork through the red goop left over from the cherry filling, and I try to come up with something to say to make him agree. But then he says, "Whatever," which is pretty close to a yes for J. R.

Dad smiles too and looks at Mom. "All right. Mom? What are your thoughts?"

Mom looks at me like she's going to say no and my heart starts beating fast. I can hear the beat swooshing in my ears. "To be honest, I'm worried about the repercussions. I don't think J. R. or Tina are quite old enough to understand what might happen if we go through with this. Tina, you need to be very sure that you want to play badly enough, that this is worth what may be said or done when your father and I are not around. No one is telling you not to play hockey. You can still play pond hockey with your friends and you have your net outside. You can skate with me at the rink. Is it really so important to play on a team?"

"Yes," I say as sure as I can. "A team that has practices and learns how to make plays and gets better at hockey."

Dad reaches across the table to put his large hand over mine. It's warm and heavy. "Tina, standing up for what you think is right is not always easy. I think this is one of those times. But I do believe you are right."

My eyes get teary again and I don't know why because it sounds like we're going to fix it after all. "I just want to play hockey," I say for the hundredth time, it feels like.

Mom nods and says, "Okay, then. If that's what you want, we'll do what we can to support you. What's next?"

Dad starts talking to Mom, but I don't pay attention. All that matters is I'm going to play hockey.

CHAPTER 9

Waiting
(December 1977)

SHARI IS USING J. R.'S STICK, SO IT'S TOO LONG for her. I pass her the tennis ball and she whacks the stick at it. The blade hits the ground with a terrible cracking sound and misses the ball completely.

"You have to keep your eye on it," I say, trying to remember all the early stuff Dad told me to make my shot better.

"I'm trying," Shari says. "It's not the same as hitting a baseball. I can do that." But she's not really trying. Not that hard.

"Here, get ready," I say, dribbling a second tennis ball back and forth with my stick. She stands the way I showed her, with both hands on the stick and her knees a little bent. The top of the stick pokes out above her elbow. Yup, way too long. I bat the ball toward her and she swings the stick at it again. The stick hits the ground with a *thwack!* and the ball rolls past the stick to her feet.

"Hey!" J. R. yells from the porch. I hadn't heard him come out. "You're going to break my stick!" He jumps over the railing onto the driveway.

Shari's face turns red and she lays the stick down on the ground where she's standing. "Sorry, I didn't mean to. Tina said I could use it, I wasn't trying to break it. I just…I just…." She stops talking and looks at her mitts, pulling at a loose string sticking out of the top of one.

"She's not going to break it, J. R. We're just shooting on the net," I say. J. R. walks toward the stick, picking it up as if it were made of glass. He runs his hand down the shaft, looking at it closely. "It's not broken, spaz," I say.

J. R. turns to glare at me. "It's too long for her. I heard her whacking it off the ground."

"Whatever. You hit it off the ground harder than that when you miss the net!" J. R. doesn't say anything back, he just takes his stick and walks toward the garage. He'll probably hide it so I can't use it.

Shari takes a couple of steps backward and says, "I should probably go home now anyway."

"Really? We could do something else," I say. It's still a long time till supper, and it'll be boring if she leaves. "Wanna go climb the tree in the field? Or we could build a fort. Or go get some O-Pee-Chee cards? Or go in and play a game? I just got Life this weekend."

"Nah, I really gotta go," Shari says. "Bye." She turns and heads down our driveway.

"See you later, Alligator!" I shout after her, but she doesn't do the crocodile part. I could walk home with her to fill some time, but I don't. Instead I go into the house.

My room is at the top of the stairs. My Sabres poster is on the biggest wall. The corners got a bit torn moving it from our old house. I wanted to paint the room blue and yellow to match the poster, but Mom said I should stick to white. I carry my shoebox of hockey cards to the bed and sit down, pull out a pile, and start to flip through them.

When a flock of birds swoops past, it catches my eye and I look out the window. The field is covered in snow since it's December and the sun is bright off the white. I can't even see the pond because the snow is covering it too. Not a pond. A puddle. Maybe when the ground thaws I can go out and dig the pond bigger, big enough to skate on it. I wouldn't need very much more space to practice stickhandling and shooting. I don't need a big pond to play a real game on because by then I'll be playing in the rink. Hopefully.

Dad went and talked to the Human Rights Act people last week. It's called a complaint, which is funny because Mom is always telling me not to complain. I guess some things are worth complaining about. I wanted to go with him, but he said it would be too boring for me. When he got home from work that day he looked tired; his hair was messy and his tie was loosened. He sank into his chair and put his head back and closed his eyes, so even though I wanted to ask him a million questions about what happened and when I get to play, I didn't. I waited. I thought he'd tell me. But he didn't. He didn't say anything through supper about it, and by the time Mom was cutting the pie for dessert, I was starting to worry that maybe it hadn't gone well. Finally I couldn't take it anymore and said, "Dad? Did they say I could play?"

He looked like he was surprised I asked, which is weird because it's all I talk about these days. Even Mom had told me, "Tina, you're preaching to the choir. I agree you should get to play, so you don't need to convince me. We can talk about other stuff for a change, eh?"

"The Human Rights people, did they say I could play?" I said.

He smiled, and it wasn't a sorry-we-tried kind of smile. But then he shook his head. "I'm sorry, Tina, you must have misunderstood. It's not decided by them or right now. What I did today was file a complaint explaining why we think there's been discrimination. Now they will decide if the Human

Rights Act applies. If so, they have to appoint a lawyer to take it to court. It'll take time for them to gather the information they need to make a case, and the hockey association will need time to build their defence—their side of the story. And then they'll have to find a date that works for the lawyers and the judge. It will be some months yet before it goes to court."

The whole time he was talking I could feel my middle get heavy, like I swallowed something thick and hard that was slow to go from my mouth down into my stomach. Dad was looking at me and all I could say was, "Oh."

"I'm sorry, honey, I thought you understood. I should have been more clear explaining the process." Dad reached across the table to put his large hand on my shoulder. It was warm and heavy, making me feel safe. I forced my mouth to smile.

"But they're going to get the lawyers and go to court and make them let me play?" I asked.

Dad nodded. "Well, they agree that not allowing you to play because you're a girl could be considered discrimination under the new Human Rights Act. They agreed to fight it in court."

My stomach felt a little better, a little lighter.

So, next year. I look at my favourite card, the René Robert all-star team card. I like the yellow stripes on his socks. They look smart against the Sabres blue. Maybe my jersey will be blue and yellow like the Sabres. Next year is forever away, but it's a little better than never.

CHAPTER 10

Only Girls Clean the Boards
(December 1977)

M RS. BOUDREAU ASKS SHARI TO STAY AND
clean the boards for her, so I stay to help too.
I'd have to wait anyway to walk home with her, and
waiting is more boring than cleaning the boards. We
go to the girls' bathroom to get wet paper towels
and carry them back to the room, careful not to let
them drip too much in the hall. Shari is taller than
me, so she stands on a chair to reach the top of the
board and I wipe down the bottom half. Drips from
her paper towel run down the board, leaving black

lines behind. I rub my paper towel across the surface, hiding the black lines in a smear of grey. Another wipe darkens the grey swipe and a third leaves it black as we erase all the chalk marks Mrs. Boudreau made throughout the day.

"What are you doing this weekend?" Shari asks from the chair above.

"I dunno," I say. "Mom has a practice tonight, so I'll probably go skating then. Do you want to come? I could see if you could."

"Nah. I'm not a good skater," Shari says. "But maybe you could come over tomorrow?"

"Sure, I'll ask." I finish wiping my part of the board. I'm faster, because Shari has to step off the chair and move it over each time she can't reach any farther. I take the board erasers and pound the two together over the garbage bin. White chalk dust falls like snow into the bin, lining the creases of the black bag with drifts of white.

"We're done!" Shari says to Mrs. Boudreau when she's wiped the last of the top. She lifts the chair and turns it upside down on the desk closest to the board.

Mrs. Boudreau stands up and walks over to study the board. She looks it over as if to find a spot we've missed. "You've done a decent job, thank you. Have a good weekend and don't forget to study your spelling list."

I try not to run out of the classroom to my hook in the hall, but I can't wait to get out of the school.

In the hall I swap my sneakers for my winter boots and pull my hat and mitts from the sleeve of my jacket.

"Are you going sledding?" Chris asks behind me. I didn't see him coming, but I know his voice by now.

I turn around, but Shari answers first. "No, we were cleaning the boards. What about you?"

"Yeah, sledding on the hill," Chris answers, then turns to me. "But I should've guessed you guys were here cleaning boards since that's a job for girls." He snarls the last word.

"Is not!" I say before I remember my decision to ignore him and all the other guys bugging me.

"Is too. Why do you think Mrs. Boudreau never asks a boy to do it, huh?" He doesn't wait for my answer, he turns and runs down the hall crashing into the door so fast that it swings open on the hinges and catches in the wind, banging backward, then slams closed.

Is that true? I can't remember Mrs. Boudreau asking any of the boys to stay behind. It *is* true. She asks the boys to go get the janitor when someone spills glue or a drink at lunch and she asks them to hand out the heavy boards when we do art class on Fridays.

"I never noticed that," I say to Shari as we walk toward the door, bundled and zipped up for the cold outside.

"Noticed what?" Shari says. She takes her lip balm out of her purse and rubs it on her lips.

"That Mrs. Boudreau only asks the girls to clean the boards. Why do you think that is?"

Shari shrugs, her scarf lifting up and down on her shoulders. "Probably doesn't want to be bothered with having any of those boys staying after school," she says, laughing.

I laugh too. That could be it. Stepping outside, the wind swipes the breath from my mouth and for a second I can't breathe. I hate that feeling. I clamp my mouth shut and take a deep breath in that feels cold right through my nose into my chest. Shari and I turn to head home and walk past the hill where there are lots of kids sledding. They take turns, some waiting at the top of the hill, others walking up, others sliding down until they topple off on the field below. It does look like fun, but I told Mom I'd be home after school and I didn't bring my sled.

Chris and Andy are standing at the top of the hill waiting their turn to go down. "See ya, Tony!" he yells after me. I don't turn around, but I can hear him and Andy laugh.

"Don't worry about them," Shari says. Before I can respond there's a yell behind us that makes us both turn around.

J. R. is standing at the top of the hill by Andy, and Chris is pushing himself out of the snowbank. Snow clings to the threads of his hat and bunches in his scarf against his neck. He pulls his mitten off to scoop the snow out of his scarf. "What was that for?" he yells at J. R.

"Knock it off," J. R. says, then leaves Chris standing there trying to brush the snow off.

J. R. trots toward us with his head down. When he gets close I say, "J. R., thanks, but I—"

"I didn't do it for you," J. R. barks. He stops and stands facing me, too close and too tall. "I'm sick of it and it's only getting started. All because you want what you want. Do you ever think of how this affects the rest of us?"

"Yes," I say in a small, quiet voice. But he doesn't wait to hear my answer; he's already turned and run off toward home.

Shari puts her arm through mine and pulls so I start walking, linked with her. The wind is cold, and I don't know if my eyes are watering because of that or because they're tears.

"He doesn't mean it," Shari says.

"Yes, he does."

"Well, brothers are jerks," she says again. "I know: I have three of them."

I laugh for Shari because she's trying to cheer me up, but it's not very loud or very real sounding.

"Don't worry about them," she says again, and I don't know who she means—the guys, or J. R., or someone else? "I think it's good you're trying to change the rules."

"You do?" She nods so I ask, "Do you want to play too?"

Shari laughs, but her laugh is real and loud and makes me laugh for real too. When she stops, she says, "I'm not a good skater, remember? And you've seen how I try to shoot on the net. I'll stick to baseball."

CHAPTER 11

Christmas Surprise!
(December 1977)

ILOVE CHRISTMAS. LOVE IT. MOM PUTS Christmas records on and the house always smells like cookies. Some people make a gingerbread house, but my mom makes a gingerbread town! She makes houses and people and buildings and even a rink where the gingerbread people can skate and play hockey. Sometimes I help her make pieces for the town. This year I made a gingerbread version of me shooting on a net beside a house.

Last year all I wanted for Christmas was hockey skates—to play hockey when I turned ten. That was the only thing on my list. I have them all broken in for hockey now and I wear them at the rink when Mom's teaching. I even take my stick just in case. I hope they're not too small when I finally get to play on a team. If I ever do.

When I walk into the kitchen after school, Mom is standing at the sink washing up a few dishes. "Guess what I found while I was unpacking," she says.

"What?" I ask, pouring myself a glass of milk.

"Take a look!" she says, nodding her head toward the end of the counter.

Under some folded tea towels is a thick, glossy Sears catalogue. "The *Wish Book*! You found it!" I say, pulling it out from under the cloths. I take it back to the table and start flipping through the colourful pages full of Christmas gift suggestions.

"It was in one of the kitchen boxes. Here," Mom says and I look up. She's holding a pen out to me. "Don't forget your initials."

I take the pen and flip back to the beginning of the catalogue. J. R. and I have marked up the *Wish Book* for as long as I can remember. Before I could write, I'd point to things and he'd write a "T" in for me. Last year I looked through it but didn't circle anything other than the skates, to make sure Mom and Dad knew how serious I was about getting them. It was only a couple of weeks ago I asked Mom where the catalogue was, and she said it must've gotten thrown out in the move.

I flip through the clothes quickly. Who wants clothes for Christmas? But those jeans with the bright stripes on the back pockets are far out. I circle the jeans and add a "T." I slide through the underwear and tools, past the page of Farrah Fawcett beanbag chairs, until the page opens to a spread of Atari cartridge video games. That would be so fun. I circle the Atari, add a "T," and then go through the games. I should only circle two; I don't want to look greedy. I settle on Super Pong and Speedway and then flip the page over in case I change my mind. The next few pages have electronic sports games. The figures shake to move the ball from one place to another until a team scores. I think playing the real sport would be better than that. A pinball machine for $645? Who would put a pinball machine in their house? And who would pay that much for it? I circle it and write "J. R." in my best imitation of his handwriting, trying not to laugh loud enough for Mom to hear me.

She comes over with a plate of cookies and says, "Did you find anything interesting?"

"Yeah, there's some cool things," I say, but I don't show her any of my circles. Not yet. She smiles at me and puts the plate down in front of me. Chocolate chip. They're still my favourite, even though they're not exactly a Christmas cookie. I pick the roundest one and bite into it. Warm and sweet. "Thank you," I say with my mouth full of cookie.

"You're welcome," Mom says and puts her hand on my head for a second before she goes back to the counter. "What shall we have for supper?" She's not really asking me. She's talking to herself.

A few pages later there are record players. They all look at the same to me, I don't know why the prices are so different. I circle the picture of ten 45s for $1.99 including Elton John, ABBA, the Beatles...that would be good. A few pages later there's a spread of board games. I don't like the strategy or war ones, and there's not much else; Arab–Israeli Wars? Victory in the Pacific? WarpWar? No thanks.

But Star Wars is different. I circle two action figures and one of the Millennium Falcon models, then close the book. What I really want isn't in this catalogue anyway. I probably have just enough time to get in some shots before I need to set the table for Mom. "I'm going outside," I say as I head out of the kitchen.

"Don't go far, supper is in twenty minutes," Mom shouts after me.

"I'll be in the driveway," I say as I'm stuffing my feet into my boots.

Dad pulls into the driveway when I'm on shot eighty-seven. Or ninety-seven. I lost track. I stop shooting and go open his door as he gathers his briefcase and some mail from the passenger seat.

"Hello, Tina," he says.

"Hi, Dad."

"How was your day? How was school?"

"Good." I step back as he gets out of the car. "Wanna shoot some?"

He smiles at me. "Sure. Let me put these things inside." He walks toward the house and I go to the garage to get his stick out of the pile of hockey sticks in the corner. It's the longest one. I grab it at the handle and pull until it comes loose from the sticks leaning against it. Two fall to the floor with a clattering sound. I pick them up and stuff them back in the corner pile.

I put his stick over the top of the net and have time to take five more shots before he comes out. He's still dressed in his suit and overcoat. His galoshes are stretched over his shiny shoes, but they are unzipped. He has rolled up the legs of his pants and traded his fancy gloves for a thick pair of knit mittens. He looks silly.

"Don't laugh," he says. "I can still beat you in best of ten."

We take turns shooting—him, then me, then him, then me. When he shoots I go get the balls that missed and pass them back to where he's standing so we have more to shoot. He misses three but hits the net on seven. I'm shooting my last ball—I've missed two already—so this one's for the win.

"Take your time," he says. He always says that. But hockey is a fast game. If I ever get on a real team,

I won't be able to take my time and make the shot perfect. So I shuffle the ball back and forth and then look up and shoot fast. It misses the net wide, just by an inch or two. "Tie!" Dad says as if he's excited it ended that way. He reaches out his hand and I shake it. Next time I'll win.

"Hey Tina, I have some news," he says when I go to get the ball from under the bushes.

"What?"

"I was talking with Mr. Houghman this afternoon. He's the gentleman hired by the Human Rights Committee to present your case in the court?" He says this like a question, making sure I know who he's talking about, so I nod. I can't say anything; I'm holding my breath. "And he has arranged it so that you may play while we wait on the courts to come to a final determination."

What did he just say? Dad's big lawyer words get in the way sometimes, but I'm pretty sure he said I get to play. "What?" I ask, to make sure I heard him right.

He laughs a little and says, "I've arranged with you to play on Jim Ross's team. You'll start after Christmas."

"Really?" I say. I mean, it would be really mean to be teasing right now, but I sort of can't believe it.

"Really." He's smiling, and it's not a trickster smile. "For now it's temporary, until we can go to court and get the association to change the rules, but you can play and—"

"Far out!" I shout and run toward him. I crash into him and he catches me, lifts me off the ground, and spins me around. I think of the Sears Wish Book. All the Ts I marked earlier suddenly seem silly. Who wants 45s and action figures? Getting to play hockey will be the best Christmas present ever!

CHAPTER 12

Coach Jim
(December 1977)

WHEN I WAKE UP IT'S SNOWING. IT'S BEEN three days since Christmas, but the best day of Christmas vacation is finally here. My first practice with my team. My team. A real team at the rink. It's snowing, but not hard enough to keep us home. I hope.

I head down to the kitchen, where Dad is making fried eggs. "Want a sandwich?" he asks me.

"Yes please," I say, sliding into my chair.

"You ready?" I know he's asking about the practice; that's all there is to talk about. At least to me.

"Yup!" I say. I'm ready. But even as I say it there's

a little fluttery feeling in my belly. I don't want him to know I'm nervous. What if he thinks being nervous means I'm not ready?

But then he says, "It's okay to be nervous." How does he know that's what I was thinking?

Maybe my face looks nervous. I smile at him. "I'm not," I say, but my voice does that dumb shaky thing.

He looks at me for a moment and I feel my face getting hot. He says, "Okay, good then. But if you were nervous, that would be okay and totally normal." He messes up my hair and puts a plate down on the table in front of me. There's a fried egg and jam between two pieces of toast. My favourite breakfast. "Eat up. Eggs are good for your endurance."

The road is snowy, but the plow has already been out to clear it. Dad drives more slowly than usual, but we still make it to the rink early. Dad lifts my bag out of the trunk and puts it on his shoulder.

"I'll take it," I say.

"You sure?"

"Yeah, I got it." He helps lift it onto my shoulder. The weight presses down on me, and I stumble a bit but catch myself and walk toward the rink.

Dad holds the door open and I enter. The lobby is noisy with people walking in and out. There are groups of people standing and talking over hockey bags dumped on the floor. Three little kids are playing chase around the adults and bags. I stop. Dad bumps into me.

"Move in, Tina, keep going," he says. I step forward a bit, but I don't know which way to go. It's not like I haven't been here before. But when I skate with Mom, I tie my skates on the bleachers. I know the dressing rooms are down the hall over there, but which dressing room is my team in? Dad walks around me, and I follow him farther into the lobby and stand behind him while he approaches a man I don't recognize. They're talking, but I can't hear what they're saying. I look around. The lobby has gotten more quiet. The kids are still running and screeching, but the grown-ups aren't talking anymore. Most of them are looking at me. One woman leans close to the woman beside her and whispers in her ear. They both laugh and one shakes her head. Suddenly my face is burning hot, even though it's cold in here. Maybe it wasn't such a good idea to eat that egg sandwich. It feels squirmy in my stomach.

Dad turns to me then and says, "Come on, Tina. You can get dressed over here." I follow him, but he's not headed to the dressing rooms—he's headed to the stands. There is a game being played on the ice and people are cheering and yelling from the seats. Dad stops at the closest end of the stands. "Here we go," he says and takes my bag from me. He puts it on the floor and unzips the zipper. I don't get it.

"What? Which dressing room are we in?"

"Your team is in four, and you can meet up with them on the ice in a bit. You can get dressed here."

"Here?" I still don't get it. "Why can't I—" But as I'm speaking I figure it out. It's a boys' team and a boys' dressing room. Why didn't I think of that before?

"Next time we'll get you dressed at home, but this time, we'll just be quick," Dad says, pulling out my shin guards. "Hurry now, before you get cold."

It is cold. But I take off my jacket and new Muppets sweater and then my pants until I'm only in my shorts and T-shirt. I try not to shiver. Dad steps forward to put my shin guard on my leg, but I take it from him. "I can do it."

"Right. Of course you can," he says and smiles. I put on the equipment as quickly as I can: shin guards, socks, pants, skates (I tie those myself too), shoulder pads, Sabres jersey (from Santa for my real hockey practices), elbow pads. By the time I'm dressed the Zamboni is cleaning the ice.

A man walks up to Dad with his hand stretched out to shake. "Hi, Mr. Forbes? I'm Jim Ross."

"Call me Rob, please. This is Tina."

The man smiles down at me and puts his hand out again. I take off my hockey glove and shake his hand. It's warm and he squeezes tightly. "Hi Tina, I'm Coach Jim. Are you ready to play?"

"Yes, sir," I say.

"She's excited," Dad says and Coach Jim turns back to him. Dad lowers his voice but I can still make it out. He says, "I want to thank you for accepting her on your team."

"We're happy to have her," Coach Jim says. He looks at me. "I've seen you here skating. You're quick." I don't know what to say to that, so I nod. They both laugh and my face feels warm in spite of the cold rink. Thank goodness the Zamboni is done. I stand up, put on my helmet, and walk toward the door in the boards. I just want to get on the ice. I don't like not knowing what to say and having everyone looking at me, whispering and shaking their heads. But when I get on the ice, I'll know what to do. I pull up on the latch, but it doesn't budge. Coach Jim reaches in front of me and opens the door. He taps on my helmet and says, "Go get 'em!"

I step on the ice. It's smooth. So smooth that I glide forward easily just by pushing my back foot off the rubber on the other side of the door. I keep my head down and skate once around the ice, watching the blue and red lines slip under my skates. The other players skate past me, cutting the ice with their pushes. I push a bit harder, picking up speed, and lean into the crossovers in the corner. The cold air blows on my face. I'm flying.

A whistle blows. Coach Jim is standing by the bench with his stick in the air, whistle in his mouth. I skate toward him and join the other players taking a knee in front of him. Chris slides in beside me on one knee. I should've known he'd be on this team.

He hisses "Hey, Tony!" in my ear, just loud enough for me to hear and no one else. I make sure to stare right at the coach.

"Team, we have a new player. This is Tina." He points his stick at me, but he didn't need to. They all knew I was there already, and they know me from school. Half of them were already looking at me instead of him while he talked. I just keep staring at the coach. "I expect you all to make her feel welcome. We are a team and she is part of it now." The coach *tap-tap-tap*s the blade of his hockey stick on the ice and the players copy him. The slapping sounds ricochet around the rink. "All right, have a look up here. We're going to run that drill that we started last practice, remember? It was before all the turkey and Christmas presents, so I wouldn't be surprised if it's been pushed out of your memories. Have a look. We'll have the defence here...." The coach uses a marker to write on his whiteboard, Xs and lines and arrows to show where we are to start and go and stop. My heart races a little. This is happening.

I line up with the forwards behind the goal line, ready to carry the puck up the ice. When it's my turn, I skate up and fall in with two other skaters. David and Chris. David passes to Chris, who passes it back to him. I skate wide along the boards, waiting for my turn. David passes it to me, and it lands on my stick. I cut into the middle and look to pass to Chris. He slaps his stick on the ice and I send it his way, hitting his stick right on the tape. I follow the pass to the boards and Chris cuts in, passes it to David. I slip over the blue line, careful to stay behind the puck as David cuts into the middle. He slides it over to me and I head toward the net. Chris is slapping his stick on the ice again. Hard. He calls my name. But we're close enough to the net; I can shoot it from here. I pull back and slap it high over the goalie's right shoulder. It hits the netting and falls behind him. I try to act cool but I can't help but smile.

I skate to the back of the line to wait my turn again. There are three lines, so I don't know why Chris is coming to line up behind me. For a second I remember what he said on the soccer field: Why don't you go play jump rope with the girls where you belong? He stops behind me and I clench my teeth so I won't say something rude back to him when he tells me I shouldn't be here playing hockey. I glare at him too.

"You should've passed! That was my shot!" he says, then skates away and joins another line. I may get to play for now, but I guess that hasn't changed everything.

CHAPTER 13

Black Diamond
(January 1978)

CHRISTMAS BREAK IS ALWAYS TOO SHORT. It went by so fast, and now it's the first day back to school. Getting up early today isn't so hard because we had two more practices to get up for. I was up early a lot even though it was a holiday. I'm dressed in my new jeans with the patches on the butt and my *Charlie's Angels* T-shirt, and I'm in the kitchen for breakfast before Mom calls up to me a second time.

"Good morning, Tina, how did you sleep?" she asks.

"Good," I say and sit in my chair. She puts a plate in front of me with some scrambled eggs and bacon. I lift a piece of bacon up and bite the end off. It's salty.

"Use your fork, please," Mom says. Right. I find my fork under the edge of the plate and use it to scoop some egg and a piece of bacon and put them in my mouth. Mom goes into the hall and calls up the stairs for J. R. to hurry up, then comes back, touching the top of my head as she goes. "Are you ready to go back to school?"

I shrug. Sure I'm ready, but given the choice, who wouldn't want to stay on vacation? Sledding, snow fights, skating—and this year, hockey!

"Would it cheer you up if I told you we found out when your first game is?"

"Yes! When is it?"

She walks to the calendar on the wall and looks at January. I race around the table to stand beside her.

"Sunday," she says, pointing to the square where 'Tina Game, 11:00' is written in her neat handwriting. Sunday!

"And when's my next practice?" I answer my own question by pointing at the square where she wrote 'Tina Practice, 3:00.' Saturday. Four days away.

"I'm coaching after, so I'll get to watch some of your practice. Dad said you are doing well." She puts her hand on my shoulder for a second and then says, "Now hurry and eat your breakfast up before it gets cold."

I nod and sit at the table, scoop a bacon-and-egg forkful into my mouth. Our practices so far have been good. Easy, really. The drills are simple and easy to skate through. I can score on the goalie whenever I try, though I do make sure to hit his pads sometimes. No one likes a show-off, after all. I also make sure I sometimes come second or third in the sprints. When I skate my fastest I can finish first.

No one says anything bad, not even Chris. One time this boy Jason skated past me and bumped my shoulder. Maybe it was an accident, though. Coach Jim is nice. He always comes out of the dressing room when the boys are dressed and tells me to come in while he goes over the drills on his whiteboard. I get dressed at home now. Everything except my skates, gloves, and helmet. It makes it kind of hard to tie my skates with all my top gear on, but that's getting easier too.

J. R. comes into the kitchen and sits at the table beside me.

"You need to eat quickly, J. R. It's almost time to go," Mom says. "Where are your socks?"

J. R. has already stuffed a whole bacon strip in his mouth, without using his fork. "I couldn't find any clean ones," he says, mouth full.

"That hasn't stopped you from wearing them before," Mom says before she walks out of the kitchen. She keeps talking, but not loud enough for us to hear what she says. J. R. continues to stuff his bacon in his mouth, strip after strip, until it's all gone.

"Gross," I say. "Use your fork at least."

He laughs, then looks at me and chews, opening his mouth wide between each chew. A few bacon crumbs fall out. "See food!" he says.

Ugh, the "Do you like seafood" joke. I hate it. "J. R., you're disgusting," I say. I'm done my breakfast, so I can get away from him. I put my empty plate in the sink. I hurry through brushing my teeth, packing my backpack, and getting dressed in my snow gear.

"Bye, Mom," I shout into the house, not knowing where she is exactly.

She comes out of the kitchen drying her hands on a tea towel. "Wait for your brother, Tina."

"But he'll make me late! It's time to go and I want to walk with Shari. She'll be leaving soon."

"Wait for your brother," she says again.

It's hot in the house with my winter clothes on. I can feel sweat starting to trickle from the back of my head down my neck. "But I'm ready and it's hot in here," I say.

"Tina," she says. She means business.

"Fine. I'll wait outside," I say, pushing the door open and stepping out onto the porch as she yells my brother's name up the stairs.

I put my bag on the step and pick up my stick from the side of the net, then fish a ball out from under the netting. I pass it back and forth on the blade, then lift a wrist shot into the top right corner. Fish the ball out again. Pass, pass, pass, shot top left. Fish, pass, pass, pass, pass, top right...I make eleven shots and miss four before J. R. finally comes out onto the porch, pulling his hat onto his head.

"Come on, Tina! You're going to make us late!" he yells as he runs past me down the driveway.

"J. R.! Wait!" I yell after him, but he doesn't slow down. I drop my stick, grab my bag, and run after him.

Shari has already left, but we're not late for school. The schoolyard is still full of kids when we get there. J. R. takes off to another corner, where his dopey friends are throwing snowballs at each other. I walk through groups of kids looking for some of my friends. I find Shari sitting on a bench by the door with Lindsay.

"Hi," Shari says when I walk up. "Sorry I didn't wait. Mom said I'd be late."

"It's okay," I say, sitting beside her. "I was ready, but Mom made me wait for J. R." Shari nods. She has a brother too, so she knows how annoying they are.

"My dad drove me," Lindsay says.

So what? I don't like Lindsay much. She always tries to make herself sound better; better clothes, better toys, better everything. I don't know why Shari is friends with her. "Anyway, like I was saying," Lindsay says, but she stops there and doesn't even get on with what she was saying.

"Lindsay was telling me about her trip. They went skiing over the break," Shari says to me.

"Fun!" I say. I'd love to go on a ski trip. Dad says maybe someday when he's not so busy at work.

"It was fun," Lindsay says. "And this year I went by myself on the diamond slope. I was the youngest one on the chair lift. Even the operator asked me if I was sure I was allowed up there. I didn't tell him that I'm not, of course. Dad would have a conniption if he knew I went on it. I don't get it. Dad takes my brother on them and he's younger than me, but he never takes me. Says I'm not strong enough. So I went by myself."

That's not fair, I think. It's like me not being able to play hockey. I'm glad my mom and dad aren't the ones telling me I can't play; it must be tough to have your own dad think that you can't do something just because you're a girl.

"Were you scared?" Shari asks. She hasn't been skiing, I don't think.

"Not a bit," Lindsay says and laughs. "And you should have seen the ski lodge! It was huge, with all these fancy dishes and glasses and an enormous fireplace and free hot chocolate and waiters who brought us anything we asked for. I wish I could live there all the time." She stops for a minute and makes a face like when someone on TV is feeling all dreamy. Ugh, so fake. "Anyways, what did you do, Tina?"

I shrug. I don't really want to follow her Christmas vacation story with mine. Suddenly sledding and snow forts seem boring and babyish.

"Tina played hockey," Shari said.

"So? Tina is always playing hockey," Lindsay says, laughing.

"No, no, real hockey. She's on a team now."

Lindsay stops laughing and looks at me. I don't like the way her mouth is curled up on one side. Dad would call it a smirk.

"It's true. I'm on the Leafs. I've been to three practices and have another one on Saturday. We have a game on Sunday."

"They let you play?" she says.

"Sure, why not?" I ask. I can feel my fingernails pinching into my hands from my fists being so tight inside my mittens. My face is warm, even though it's cold outside.

"You're a girl," Lindsay says. As if I didn't know that already. As if she didn't just brag about doing the ski hills even though her dad said she couldn't. What's the difference?

"So?" I say. Lindsay looks at me for a moment, then looks at Shari. No one says anything. For a moment her smirk goes away and she looks like she's thinking about something sad. Then she bursts out laughing. I'm not sure what's funny.

"Well, for one, hockey is for boys and it's a boys' team. I guess if you want to be a boy...."

"Girls can play hockey," I say, but she's already standing up.

She stands there staring at me for a second, but it's like she's looking somewhere far away, not seeing me at all. She laughs again, though it sounds kind of fake, and shakes her head like she can't believe what I'm saying. Her high ponytail swings back and forth behind her head. "Catch you on the flip side, Shari," she says, and when she turns away I think she says, "chump." That's probably for me.

I look at my mittens. My hands are balled up into fists inside them so the tops of the mittens are empty and floppy.

"Don't listen to her," Shari says.

I shake my head. "I'm not," I say. And I'm not, really. Who cares what stupid Lindsay says? I like hockey and I get to play. I don't care if she thinks it's weird.

"I think she's jealous," Shari whispers, as if other kids might overhear, even though no one is close enough or paying attention.

I bet my eyes do that surprised thing that Lindsay's were doing a minute ago. "Of what?" I ask.

"Of you, and that your parents help you do what you want. Her dad doesn't even let her go on the tricky hills, and he lets her little brother. I bet it's because she's a girl. I bet she'd play hockey if she were allowed to."

The bell rings then before I can ask Shari what else Lindsay wanted to do but wasn't allowed. I hadn't thought of it that way. What if my parents had said I couldn't play and that was that? I'd be mad too.

Shari and I hurry to get in line to go into the school. Mrs. Kennedy stands inside the door and says, "Hello, welcome back," to each of us as we walk past her. The school is warm and bright and someone obviously cleaned everything while we were away. But I'd rather be at the rink.

CHAPTER 14

J. R. Flies Up
(January 1978)

TURNS OUT LINDSAY ISN'T THE ONLY ONE who thinks it's weird that I'm on the hockey team. I didn't know so many people would even know I was playing now, let alone care. I expected Chris to be snarly, and he is. He spends the day telling everyone who'll listen that he's way faster than me and can shoot way harder. And Kevin, who's on the Canadiens team that practices after us, keeps saying that I do the drills wrong because I don't understand them. That's not true. And when they say those things their friends snicker and look at me and laugh some more when they see me watching them. Why do they care so much?

I'm still thinking about it at supper when Dad asks, "How was school today?"

J. R. says, "Good."

"Tina?" Dad says.

"They were really bugging her today," J. R. says before I can answer. I wish he hadn't. It's no big deal, and I don't want them to think I'm bothered by a little teasing. Even if I am.

"About what?" Dad asks.

"Hockey," I say, but I quickly add, "It's no big deal, really. I can handle it."

But Dad is frowning when I look up at him. "What did people say?"

I don't mean to say much, just give one tiny example to answer his question, but once I start talking it's like I can't stop. I don't mean to cry either, but suddenly the tears and the words and all of it comes out: "Lindsay laughed at me and called me a chump and said I must want to be a boy. And Mike and Kevin kept calling me Tony all day. And Chris said I was the slowest skater on the team. And Kim said I should buzz cut my hair if I'm really a boy. And Michelle said her dad wouldn't let me play on his team and then Rick said his dad said he wouldn't either and the only coach who would let me play on their team was Coach Jim." I run out of breath. "Is that true?" I whisper.

Dad shakes his head like he's confused. "Is what true, Tina?"

92

I wipe my face with my sleeve and no more tears come out. "Is it true that Coach Jim was the only one who would let me play on his team?"

Dad takes a bite of his meatloaf and chews it. He's looking at me like he's trying to decide what to say. I don't know what there is to think about; I just want to hear the truth. "Yes," he finally says. "Coach Jim is happy to have you on his team."

"But was he the only one?" I want an answer. I don't know why I want to know, because thinking about it, wondering about it, is already making me feel kind of sick. But I want to know for sure.

Mom says, "Tina, let's not worry about this. It's really not worth—" but Dad puts his hand on her arm and she stops talking.

"Tina, we talked about this before, about how if we pushed for you to play we would make some people unhappy. We decided together that it was the right thing to do and it was worth whatever upset it caused, but now we're seeing evidence of what we talked about. If it's more than you bargained for, it's okay to stop. There's nothing wrong with stepping back if it's too much. You have nothing to prove."

He waits, and I realize he's asking me again. "I want to play," I whisper, but I can't look at him. Instead I stare at the ketchup lines on my meatloaf.

"Then you deserve to know the whole truth. You're right. Most of the coaches were not agreeable to having you play on their team. It doesn't do any good to wonder about their reasons. Let's focus on the fact that Coach Jim is happy to have you on the Leafs. He told me he saw you skate when you were on the ice with your mom and he knew you'd have a lot to contribute to the team. Let's just concentrate on that, okay?" My eyes are prickly, but I blink hard. I'm not going to cry over this. I'm not. He's right, so I nod. "Good girl," Dad says and I blink harder.

"Well, she's not the only one getting teased," J. R. says. We look at him and he's glaring at his meatloaf.

"How so?" Mom asks him.

"Mark asked me if I was going to join Brownies since Tina was playing hockey. I told him no 'cause I'd already flown up to Guides."

I can't help it. I laugh. And Mom and Dad laugh and the laughter must be catching, because we keep laughing more and more until Dad takes his glasses off and uses his napkin to wipe his eyes. At first J. R. looks at us like maybe we've all gone crazy, but after a bit he laughs a little too. And I feel a whole lot better.

CHAPTER 15

Jersey #17
(January 1978)

SUNDAY TOOK A LONG TIME TO ARRIVE, BUT finally I'm getting into my hockey gear in the living room. It's a lot warmer than getting dressed at the rink, and by the time I'm pulling my jersey over my head and trying to get it untangled from my shoulder pads, I'm sweaty.

Coach Jim gave me my jersey at practice yesterday. He held it out to me and said, "I hope you're okay with number seventeen, Tina." Number seventeen is Fred Stanfield's jersey on the Sabres. That's fine.

The jersey is blue with a white maple leaf, just like the real Leafs jerseys. Except ours have "Esso," the sponsor, on the leaf, and "YMHA" under that. My number on the back is white with blue trim. It's a real jersey and it fits perfectly.

"I'm ready!" I call out to Dad. I don't know where he is and I don't want to be late.

Dad comes out of the kitchen. He's still eating his peanut-butter sandwich. "We've got lots of time, Tina. The game doesn't start for another forty-five minutes."

"But we have to get there. And Coach Jim said to be ready for the pre-game meeting ten minutes before the game starts. And it's my first game, I can't be late!"

"You're right," Dad says, but I get the feeling he's trying not to laugh when he stuffs the rest of his sandwich crusts into his mouth. He disappears and the kitchen tap turns on and off, then he comes back, drying his hands on his pants. "Let's boogie!"

Usually I roll my eyes when he tries to use cool words like us, but I'm just happy he's ready to go. I zip up my hockey bag and put it over my shoulder. It's light with only my helmet, skates, and gloves in there, but still big and floppy, and it gets in the way when I try to step into my boots.

"Need help?" Dad asks.

"Nope, I've got it," I say. And I'm ready and headed out the door while he's still sliding on his coat.

The drive is short and we arrive at the rink with lots of time to spare. But you never know; it is winter.

By now, I'm used to the hush that happens when I walk into the lobby. The parents standing around talking always stop when I walk in, but it doesn't matter. I know where I'm going now and don't have to stop in the lobby while they look at me and whisper. I walk through to the hall with the dressing rooms. I set my bag down against the wall, out of the way, and settle in to wait until the team is dressed and ready for me to come in.

While I wait I can watch the game on the ice. They're bigger kids, faster and better than us. I like watching better kids so I can get some hints on things to try. The centre is good on this team. He dekes around the defenceman and charges the net, but the goalie is ready and comes out to meet him, smothering the puck before the skater can get a shot off. He should have gone a bit wider and backhanded the puck in behind the goalie.

"Hi, Tina." I turn to see Coach Jim approaching.

"Hi," I say back.

"Are you ready to play? First game, you must be excited."

I nod and say, "Yes, sir." Thank goodness my voice doesn't crack and it's not too silly or loud. If I talked the way I feel on the inside, Coach Jim would probably think I was looney tunes.

He smiles. He has a nice smile, wide with white teeth. His cheeks wrinkle all the way up to the sides of his eyes. "Great. I'm going to put you in as a left winger on the second line, okay? We have a few players out and that would be a good spot for you to start."

"Okay," I say.

"I'll go see how those boys are making out. They should be almost dressed. You can tie your skates up in there when they're done." He walks past me and pushes the dressing room door open. The yelling and laughing that were muffled burst out, voices billowing into the rink. "All right, settle down, settle down," Coach Jim says as the door swings shut behind him, smothering the voices again. I try to listen but can't hear any words. Suddenly I'm kind of lonely standing here. It seems like everyone else knows where to be—on the ice, in the stands, in a dressing room—and I'm left out here standing in the hall by myself.

Finally the door opens again and Coach Jim sticks his head out. "Tina? Come on in." I pick up my bag and go in. The dressing room smells like sweat. The boys are chatting and laughing, and everywhere around the room there's movement as they pull on jerseys and helmets. I sit down by the door and unzip my bag, pulling my skates out.

I bend over to tie my skate. It's easier if I hold my breath, so I hurry. Also because I have butterflies in my stomach that feel squashed when I bend over in my gear. Coach Jim lists off the lines.

"Remember, we played well against this team last game," he says. "We have to stick close to number fourteen. He's a good shot, but isn't great at carrying the puck. Challenge him if he tries to carry it, make him move, and you're likely going to have a chance to take it from him. Okay?" He looks around and some of the boys are nodding. I nod too. "Don't be afraid to take a shot on the goalie. He goes down early, so try to lift it up." I can do that. "I want to see more passing this game. Last game we had too many people trying to do it all alone. You're a team. If you play like one, you'll do much better." He looks around him at all the players. "All right, helmets on, let's go." I slip my helmet on and do up the snaps, then dig my gloves out of my bag and put them on.

The captain stands up and puts his right hand forward, and the rest of the team follows suit. I stand up too, and try to squeeze my way in between David and Chris. Chris looks at me and steps in front of me, squashing my arm between his shoulder and David's. I try to pull it back, but my glove falls off. "LEAFS ON THREE!" the captain yells, then, "ONE! TWO! THREE!"

"LEAFS!" they all yell, but I miss it because I'm trying to figure out how to get my glove out of the crowd. I step back while the boys leave the dressing room; the goalie goes first and the team follows in behind him, heading out of the dressing room. When they're gone I pick up my glove and follow. I don't even care that Chris is a jerk. I can't help but smile—I hope I don't look goofy. I'll show them. I can't wait to hit the ice.

When we step onto the ice for warmup, the parents in the stands cheer. We skate circles around the half of the ice that's our space, then shoot practice shots on the goalie. When I start skating, the butterflies in my middle go away a little bit. When the buzzer goes off, we collect the pucks into the net and two players kneel to put them in the coach's bag. The rest of us head to the bench. I fall in between Ben and Kevin, the other two forwards on my line, and wait. My heart is beating really fast and my stomach twists a bit. If this game would start already, I'd feel a lot better.

THE TEAMS LINE UP and the ref stands between the two centres, his hand holding the puck over their ready sticks. He drops it, they scuffle, the puck pops out back toward our defenceman, who passes it up to the winger, and they head down the ice.

The shifts are quick. It's less than a minute into the game when the door opens and I follow Kevin onto the ice. I skate hard to the left side, along the boards and up toward their end. Kevin carries the puck and passes it over to Ben, and I keep pace, careful not to cross the blue line before Ben and the puck. I cut in toward the net and just before I can receive the centring pass I'm hit, knocked down and sliding across the ice into the boards.

For a second I'm confused and can't figure out which direction I'm facing, but once I get back up I see I'm in the corner and the puck and all the other players are headed down to our end. I take three quick running steps to pick up speed and get back on defence, but before I can get into our end I hear "TINA!" from our bench. I look over and the coaches are waving me in.

I rush over and step off as the third line goes on, walk to the end of the forwards, and get back in line for my next shift. Coach Jim is behind me. He pats my helmet and says, "Good shift. Great hustle."

The game goes on like that. We take short, quick shifts so we can skate hard the whole time, a skate down and back one or two times before we go off to get a drink and catch our breath. They don't pass to me much. Maybe they don't pass at all. But I'm good at beating everyone to the puck when it pops loose or when they dump it, so I get to play it a lot anyway. My heart is racing and I can't stop smiling. It is so fun. By the end of the second period I'm able to get out of the way of the hits more often, but I do get knocked down quite a bit. My hip hurts a little and my elbow is sore, but I don't care.

At the start of the third period my line is out for the puck drop. I skate over to the outer line of the circle and line up beside the other team's winger.

"You suck," he says. *Ignore him. Ignore him. Ignore him.* It's hard, though. I wish they'd drop the puck already. "What are you even doing here?" the skater says. I focus on keeping my stick on the ice, watching for the ref to drop the puck. *Drop it already!* After a bazillion years, he does and I lean forward to get position, but before I can react the other player's stick swipes against and under my skates, pulling my feet out from under me. He stands there, laughs, says an ugly word I'm not allowed to say, and then skates off after the play.

I get up and skate hard back into the play, taking a pass by the boards and ducking a player as he skates toward me. I get around him toward the net. Ben centres the puck and I receive it, right on the tape, turn my wrist and flick it, aimed over the goalie's shoulder. I'm hit then, but as I fall back I see the puck lift and fly up, up, over the blocker, over the shoulder, and just over the net. I land and am back on my feet as the other team carries the puck down to our end. I skate to the bench.

"Nice shot, Tina!" Coach Jim says, tapping my helmet as I walk past. It missed. It wasn't a nice shot at all.

That was the only shot I got, and the final score was 3–2 for them. I step onto the ice and follow the other skaters to the goalie, whose head we pat before we line up to shake hands. I follow my team and tap my glove to the gloves of the other skaters. None of the players look at me, not even the kid who called me the ugly name. But it doesn't matter.

I skate off the ice and follow the team toward the dressing room, but I don't know where to go. My bag and boots are in the room, but I can't go in there if the boys are getting dressed. I stop by the door until Coach Jim comes up behind me. "Come in, Tina, and take your skates off. We'll have a quick chat before everyone gets undressed."

So I leave my stick against the wall with the rest and go in and take my helmet and gloves off, putting them in my bag. Coach Jim stands in the middle and says, "Great game, kids, great game. Please wait to get undressed while I talk." I untie my skates and loosen the laces while he talks, slipping my feet out and into my cold, loose boots. "Yes, a great game. I liked our hustle and effort out there, there was lots of hard skating. Next time, I want to see a bit more passing. There was some, but still too much carrying the puck and too much dump and chase. You guys can make good passes, I know it. I want to see you play with some confidence to do that and less hurry to get rid of the puck. Overall a great game and no reason to hang your heads over the loss. Keep playing like that and we'll see some wins come our way. Hurry up and get dressed now. Don't be late for practice Tuesday morning."

I'm already good to go, so I stand up and carry my bag out, picking up my stick by the door. Dad is there waiting for me. "Great game, Tina!" he says and I smile.

"She did great," Coach Jim says. I didn't realize he came out behind me. "She really stood in there against some big hits, and that shot was so close!" I didn't know I was worried about what Coach Jim would think about my playing, but when he says that I feel even better.

"I missed," I say. I did. I should have gotten it in. I've made that shot a million times.

"You won't miss next time," Dad says.

I believe him.

CHAPTER 16

Julia Joins the Team
(February 1978)

I THINK PEOPLE ARE GETTING USED TO ME playing. Chris and some other kids at school still say some stuff. There are a couple of kids who only call me Tony now, if there are no teachers around. But last week Ben heard our teammate Jason say it and told him to stop. He walked right over to Jason, who's, like, a whole head taller than him, and said, "Why don't you knock it off, eh?"

Jason looked down at him and for a minute I was worried he'd hit him. I didn't want anyone getting hurt on my account. I can fight my own fights. But

Jason just laughed and walked away. Ben shouted after him, "You're just jealous she can skate better than you!"

"Thanks," I said, when Ben turned back to where I was standing.

Ben smiled and said, "Well it's true," before he ran off with a couple of his friends.

"He's so sweet," Shari said. I looked at her. She was all swoony-eyed. I hit her arm and she looked back at me and blushed. "Well he is!"

So I think people are getting used to it now. And it doesn't bother me much anymore if I hear other people talking. I've been to all the practices and we've played three games. I even played centre a few times when we got into penalty trouble. It's like I'm really allowed to play. Sometimes I even forget this is just an in-the-meantime arrangement. At least, that's what Dad calls it: "An in-the-meantime arrangement while we wait to go to court so you play for good."

I still get to skate at the rink every day after school while Mom coaches. It's good practice. Now I try to remember what Coach Jim taught us in practice and keep working on that on my own. If only I could take a net on the ice and shoot, but Mom says it's too in the way.

Mom turns the car into our driveway on our way home from the rink. She and J. R. are talking about his homework. I got mine done in the dressing room before I went on the ice, but J. R. didn't. He spent the time at the rink talking with some of his friends who were there before their practice and he didn't get anything done.

"I'm just saying that you need to be more responsible with your time, J. R.," Mom says. She's trying not to yell.

"Geez, I'll get it done!" J. R. says. He's not trying as hard as her not to yell. "You don't have to worry about it. Besides, you shouldn't waste your precious time worrying about my homework. You're too busy worrying about Tina and her dumb court thing."

I'm in the back seat staying out of it. I don't know why he had to say something about me. Mom doesn't say anything for a minute, and it's the kind of quiet that makes me worried she's getting really mad. At least it's not at me. But J. R. seems worried too because he doesn't say anything else, he just stares out the window.

"J. R., that is just not true," Mom says, but he keeps looking out the window.

At the end of the driveway is a red car I haven't seen before, parked beside Dad's car. It's early for Dad to be home. Strange. I push the door open before Mom stops, and I jump out, slamming it shut behind me while Mom yells, "Tina! Be careful!"

I'm up on the porch and through the door before Mom and J. R. even get out of the car. "Hi, Dad!" I yell into the house, not knowing where he is.

He appears in the kitchen doorway. He's still dressed in his work clothes, but his tie is loosened and hanging crookedly from his collar. His suit jacket is off and his shirt sleeves are rolled up to his elbows. "Hi, Tina. Come in and meet someone, will you?"

I kick off my boots, remember to set them up straight on the mat at the last second, hang my coat on the hook, then head into the kitchen.

At the table sits a woman. She has dark hair neatly pulled back into a ponytail. She's wearing black square glasses, and when she looks up at me the light from the window flashes on the lenses. She looks kind of like Wonder Woman when she's disguised as Diana Prince. She smiles at me and stands up, then steps toward me and sticks out her hand like I'm a grown-up. "Hi, Tina. I'm Julia MacDougall. I'm a lawyer and I've been assigned to your case."

I feel a bit silly taking her hand, but I do. My hand is small in hers, but she squeezes tightly and I squeeze back, letting her shake my arm up and down a bit. "Hello, Ms. MacDougall," I say. I feel a bit queasy.

"I just wanted to come and meet you and introduce myself," she says. "I'd like it if you called me Julia. Ms. MacDougall feels too formal." She makes a face when she says that, like she's just tasted something gross and it makes me giggle. "That's better," she says.

"Tina, have a seat here with Ms. MacDougall—I mean, with Julia—and have a chat. I'll go talk with your mother." Dad pulls out a kitchen chair and I sit down, and Julia sits across from me. Dad leaves.

"I hear you've been able to play some games?" Julia asks.

"Yes," I say. I hope that doesn't mean she thinks I don't need her. "It's just an in-the-meantime arrangement."

Julia nods. "Yes, so I hear. I hope we'll be able to make it permanent. Have you been having fun?"

"Yes!" I say a little too loudly and she laughs.

"That's excellent, it really is. I've heard you're very good." I don't say anything. It's not nice to brag. My cheeks are warm. Julia takes a sip from the tea Dad must have made her and smiles at me from behind the mug. "I just wanted to meet you and go over a few things with you today," she says as she puts the mug down. "I'm not here to do any real work, I just want to give you an idea of what you can expect. And you can ask me questions. Does that sound good?"

I nod. "Yes, sounds good."

"Well, my partner and I have been appointed to your case. His name is Andrew Houghman. He's a very good lawyer. It's our job to do lots of research and talk to people and come up with all the reasons you should be allowed to play hockey. We'll get a date, and when that time comes we'll go to court and Mr. Houghman and I will tell the judge all the reasons you should play. The Yarmouth Minor

Hockey Association has hired lawyers too. They will be there to tell the judge all the reasons the league doesn't have to let you play."

"Are they good?" I don't mean to interrupt, but it just comes out.

"Who?"

"The lawyers the hockey league picked?"

"Oh. Yes. Mr. Alexander Rose and Mr. Peter Sloane are both good lawyers."

My stomach feels a little sick. I want them to be terrible.

"But don't worry about them, okay, Tina? Remember that Mr. Houghman and I will be working very hard for you to play. And we really do think you are right to fight for this. That is what matters, okay?"

I nod. It sounds like she believes what she's saying. It makes me feel a little bit better. I bite my thumbnail.

"Now, do you have any questions for me?" she asks.

I know I do. There are lots of things I've been wondering about. But suddenly I can't remember any of my questions. It's like I don't even know what to ask about, and I don't want to ask anything silly.

"Um," I say and think hard. "Will I go to court too?"

Julia nods. "Yes, you'll have to go before the judge and answer questions, first from us and then from the hockey association's lawyers."

It feels like my insides have jumped up into my throat. I swallow hard.

"But before that happens we'll do some practices, just like you practice plays and then do them in games. I'll show you all our questions and try to guess the questions they might ask, and you'll practice answering them all before we go to court. How does that sound?"

"Like a good idea," I say.

"Yes, it'll be easier when you have an idea what you'll say. Don't worry, we'll make sure you're ready when it's your turn to speak to the judge."

"When will it happen?" I ask.

"We're hoping to go to court as soon as possible so that this can all be decided before it's time to register for hockey next season. I really hope that next year you'll be playing and it'll be a permanent arrangement."

"Good," I say. "And maybe some other girls will want to play then." Shari's shot is getting better every time we practice. Maybe even Lindsay would want to play if she could convince her dad...and maybe then she'd be less mad.

Julia looks at me in a funny way and smiles. "Yes, Tina, that is my hope. I think you're very brave to be the first girl to take on this fight, and I have no doubt that other girls will be able to sign up and play hockey because you took this on."

That makes me feel shy again. "It's not why I'm doing this," I whisper.

"I know it's not your reason, but it will be a result of this case. Sometimes people call it 'opening doors.' You are opening the door for girls to play, just like the boys."

"I just want to play hockey," I say. That's all it's about.

Julia smiles more. Her lipstick is red and shiny. She reaches across the table and pats my hand with her palm. "I know. Let's make it happen." She stands up, holding her mug. I stand up and offer to take it, then put it in the sink. "Well, I'm going to head home now. My cat must be starving." She laughs and so I laugh too. "I will be in touch. If you have any questions about anything at all before we talk next, please call me. Your father has my phone number. Okay?"

I nod and say, "Thank you," just before she heads out the door. Dad must have been listening, because he appears in the hall and walks her to the door. I hear their voices for a moment before the door opens and shuts again. From the window I watch her walk to her red car. She turns and waves to me before she opens it and gets in, turns the car around, and drives to the end of the driveway. She turns right toward Yarmouth and disappears down the road.

CHAPTER 17

She Shoots, She Scores!
(March 1978)

HOCKEY MAKES MY SCHEDULE BUSY. School every day, with early practice before school some days. After school I do my homework at the rink and then practice my skating while Mom coaches, and by the time we get home and have supper it's nearly time for bed. Weekends are full of practices and games. I'm glad I can walk to school and home with Shari, because it's really the only time I get to see her since she doesn't skate much. We still have lots in common, like our favourite TV shows are *CHiPS* and *Donny and Marie* and our favourite singer is Donny Osmond. She says she loves baseball, so I can't wait to play on her team.

My hockey team won a couple of games in playoffs, and that means we're in the consolation final. I dress at home. Mom makes me eat breakfast even though I don't feel like it. "I feel kinda sick," I tell her.

"It's just nerves, Tina. You need to eat. It'll make you feel better," she says and makes me a fried egg sandwich. I eat it and she's right, I feel a little better once it settles in my stomach.

I've been at the door for ten minutes with my boots and jacket on when Dad is finally ready. "You're really early," he says, but he finally grabs his keys and says, "Let's boogie!" like always.

At the rink there are a lot of parents ready to watch the game. I wait outside the dressing room. It's quiet in there. I guess the other players are nervous too. Finally Coach Jim opens the door and says, "Come on in, Tina," and I get to go in and tie on my skates.

"All right, team. You know what game this is, right? This is the final!"

"It's just the consolation final," someone says. I think it was Keith. He's always a downer.

"Doesn't matter," Coach Jim says, waving his hand at him. "This is our last game. We have a really great chance to win this game and finish the season on a high. Here's our lines." Coach Jim lists the names. Yes! I'm centre on the second line! I'll play anywhere, but centre is my favourite. "Now, we've talked about it lots, team—what do I want to see you doing?"

"Passing!" I say, along with some others.

"That's right. Passing. Passing wins games. Remember, even Tina, our fastest skater, can't move as quickly as a passed puck." It's warm in the dressing room. My cheeks burn and my ears itch. "So, lots of passing. Move the puck around and work together. Be aggressive. When they have the puck, don't give them time to make a plan. Go right at them and force them to make a move more quickly than they'd like." Coach Jim is quiet for a minute. He looks around the room at all of us. "You guys are a great team. You've worked hard this year, and I'm very happy with all you've learned. Regardless of how this game ends, you should be proud of yourselves." He is looking around at all of us, and when his eyes stop on me I smile. He looks back at Will and says, "All right, Captain, let's have a cheer!"

He steps out of the way as Will steps to the centre of the room to put his glove in. I make sure I'm not anywhere near Chris when I put my hand in. "LEAFS ON THREE, ONE...TWO...THREE...."

"LEAFS!" I yell with my team.

By third period we're locked in a 2–2 tie. I'm on the boards battling to pull the puck away from another player when a big kid slides in and crashes into me. For a second I'm pinned between him and the boards, but when he skates away with the puck I fall to the ice. That one hurt. I lie still for a moment too long and a whistle blows.

The ref skates over to me as I start to sit up. "You all right, kid?" he asks.

"Yeah," I say.

Coach Jim is halfway to me on the ice. He's yelling at the ref: "They've been targeting her all game, that's the third dirty hit she's taken!" I push myself up on my feet.

"That's hockey!" the other coach yells from his bench. "If she can't take it, she shouldn't be on the ice!" His words drop into my brain like fire-hot rocks, filling it up and threatening to erupt.

"That's not hockey, Steve, and you know it!" Coach Jim yells back at him. I want to yell something too, but if I do the ref will throw me out of the game, I know it.

"Go back to your bench, Coach," the ref says. I skate faster to the bench so we can just move on and play the game. I hate it when the coaches start arguing. I wish I could argue for myself, fight for myself. I can take it. But I don't want to miss shifts for a penalty.

The ref drops the puck and the game goes on.

"You okay to go back on?" Coach Jim asks me.

My body is all right, but my eyes are burning from the fire-hot-rock anger pressing against them and trying to get out. But I say "Yes!" clearly so he doesn't have a reason to doubt my answer. Skating also helps when I'm angry. Pushing my edges, hard passes and shots with my stick, that's the best way to stop the burning in my brain.

"All right, be ready," he says. It takes a few more seconds before the play swings and the centre comes to the bench. I hit the ice at full speed and race toward the play. Back against the boards, I kick the puck loose and then pick it up on my stick, passing it in front of the net to Chris. The goalie shifts to face Chris and I come out on the other side. Chris spins and backhands the puck to me, I lift it up and over the goalie's shoulder, and it hits the back of the net.

The stands explode in cheers and I'm squeezed in a Tina sandwich by Ben and Will in a three-way hug while they pat my helmet. We break apart and I skate toward the bench with them, following Chris, to slap gloves along the bench with the rest of the team.

I can hear Mom yelling over the crowd, "WAY TO GO, TINA!" and I'm too happy to be embarrassed.

The game ends four minutes later and we win 3–2. We're all laughing and cheering as we walk from the ice into the dressing room, and when Coach Jim walks in, he yells a big "Woo-HOOO!" that echoes around the room. "Now *that* was the way to end the season!" he says when we quiet down. "What a team! Your passing was on, your plays were great. You supported the puck, you all hustled, you worked hard! Great game!" He stands with his hands on his hips for a minute and smiles at us. "Great year," he says. "Great year indeed. All right, go ahead and get dressed. Your fans are waiting." He means our parents, but it sounds cool when he says "fans."

I sit for a minute. I already have my helmet, gloves, and skates off, and my feet are sweaty in my boots, which feel too loose after my tight-laced skates. I don't want to go, but it's time. The boys need to dress and there's no place for me in here. I stand up, lift my almost empty bag up over my shoulder pad, and head out.

CHAPTER 18

A Burger and an Insult
(May 1978)

SPRING MEANS IT'S ALMOST SUMMER, AND THE start of baseball and tennis and golf and swimming and barbecues. I miss hockey, but I can still shoot on my net in the driveway. By the time next season starts I might never miss a slap shot. If I'm allowed to play, that is.

I try not to worry about it too much. As Julia says, there's nothing I can do. She comes by once in a while to tell Dad what's going on and to give me updates. It sounds like they have a good plan. She says she thinks we'll go to court in August and that should give us lots of time to work it out before registration.

For now, we're at a cottage party for Victoria Day, and a cottage party is not a place to stress. It's hot and sunny and the lake is cold when I jump in off the end of the dock. The adults are all on the lawn doing that mingling thing grown-ups do. I like it better in the water. J. R. and a couple of other boys are out in the canoe, trying to tip each other out of it. I climb out of the water up onto a rock, watching them and thawing my toes in the sun. I wish Shari had been allowed to come, but her parents made her stay home for their own party. It's boring here without a friend.

"Tina!" my mom calls. I turn to look toward the cottage. She's standing apart from the other adults and waving for me to come in. I jump off the rock and swim back until the water is beneath my waist, then wade in. "The hamburgers are ready," she says as she wraps a towel around my shoulders. "Come get one before your brother and the other boys eat them all."

I follow her to the table set up against the cottage wall. There are paper plates held down by a rock, a few bowls of salads and chips, and bottles of ketchup and mustard. I take a plate and serve myself some potato salad. I hope there are no eggs in it. I hate the way a piece of boiled eggs looks just like a piece of potato and I don't realize it's egg until I bite into it, so I'm not expecting the slippery way it slides on my teeth and tongue. Mom doesn't put egg in her potato salad, but this isn't hers. She brought the coleslaw. I take a bun and put a swirl of ketchup and a swirl of mustard inside.

I follow Mom to the barbecue, where Mr. Guthrie is standing by with the flipper. "What would you like, Tina?" he asks as he lifts the barbecue lid.

"A hamburger, please." I have a hamburger bun on my plate, after all. He lifts a burger from the grill and puts it on the bun. "Thank you," I say.

"You're welcome," he says with a smile.

I look for my mother so I can go and stand with her rather than eat alone. She's in the shade under the hemlock with Mrs. Guthrie. I walk toward them, but before I get too far, Mom's angry voice carries toward me and makes me stop. "I'm sorry you feel that way," she says.

Mrs. Guthrie is moving her hands around while she talks. There's only a little bit of wine in her glass, but it slops around and slips out over the top. It's hard to know if there's only a little left because she drank most of it or because she spilled most of it. Now that I'm paying attention, I don't have to listen carefully to hear what she's saying.

"Really, Pamela, it is disgusting how you have pushed that girl into this situation. You come here with all of your progressive big-city ideas and look down your noses at the likes of us simple, small-town people. But we're not so simple. We all know Robert is just out to make a name for himself. He's using that girl to get recognition as the big-time lawyer he thinks he is! Elizabeth told me what they call Tina at school. Has Tina told you? Surely no mother worth her salt would want her own daughter exposed to such ugly words, but you stand by and let it happen. You let your husband use that little girl for his own promotion. You Upper Canadians will do anything for a bit of publicity." She stops talking and takes a drink from her glass. I think it's already empty.

I stand still. I can feel my heartbeat on the sides of my head, *throb, throb, throbbing*, and my teeth and fists are tight. I don't know what to do. I know what I want to do. I want to go over and scream that she's wrong and stupid and mean but a lot of the other adults have stopped talking and they're sneaking peeks toward the hemlock, even if they are pretending not to. I can't blow my stack in front of all of them. And then I notice that Mr. Guthrie is standing behind me watching as well.

Mom forces a smile. I've seen that smile before. She's trying very hard to keep her temper. "If Robert wanted to advance his career with this case, he'd be the lawyer. He is not. He chose to be the father. I thank you for your concern for Tina. I'm sure it's quite sincere. Robert and I have nothing but her best interests at heart, but I appreciate knowing that other people are looking out for her as well."

Mr. Guthrie brushes my arm as he passes me and walks toward his wife. He whispers something in her ear and takes her arm, then the two of them walk away toward the front door of the cottage. I turn to watch them go. I shouldn't stare, but I'm kind of frozen. It would be simple if my eyes could shoot energy beams like Cyclops from the X-Men and Mrs. Guthrie and her nasty words would be dust. When the Guthries disappear inside I realize I'm holding my breath. Something touches my shoulder and I jump, startled.

"Are you okay, honey?" It's Mom, her hand on my shoulder.

"Sure," I say. *I'm fine, I'm fine*, I tell myself to make my burning cheeks cool down and my stomach stop flip-flopping. Maybe I should go back in the lake.

"Good. I'm sorry you saw all that," she says, but I shake my head like it doesn't matter.

Suddenly I want to be by myself. I want to get away from everyone, even Mom. "I forgot coleslaw," I say and walk away from her back to the table. I put a spoonful of coleslaw on my plate, careful not to let it touch the burger, and walk over to a large rock on the edge of the lawn. I can feel people staring at me. It's like I'm walking through a room of cameras. If I just keep my head down and don't look back at anyone, maybe they'll all stay away.

I sit on the rock and push the potatoes around on my plate, poking each piece to see if the fork goes in easily like a piece of egg or a bit slowly like potato. I'm not hungry, but so long as I'm busy with the food, maybe people will leave me alone.

I don't get why people don't understand. I'm not telling people what to do or looking for attention or to cause trouble. We talked about how I might get teased, but I didn't know people would think bad things about Mom and Dad just because I'm trying to play. My stomach feels cold and heavy.

Maybe if I eat something my stomach will feel better. I push the salads together and try to take a bite of the burger. It doesn't work. My stomach jumps up into my throat so I stop trying. I'm hot again, from sitting in the sun. Maybe I will feel better if I go back in the water. I stand up and walk across the yard to throw my plate out and then suddenly my mom is beside me. I don't know where she came from.

"Hi, Tina. How was your dinner?"

"Good," I say. I already feel so guilty about people blaming Mom and Dad that a little lie doesn't make a difference. Sometimes lies help save someone's feelings. She doesn't say anything else and I feel weird standing there with my plate. "I'm going to go back in the water," I say, since she's not saying anything.

"All right," she says, but before I can move Mrs. Guthrie walks up to us. She is holding her hands together, twisting her fingers. Her face is pink.

"Pamela, do you have a moment?" she says. Mom

nods, but Mrs. Guthrie looks at me and then back to Mom. "A moment to speak privately?"

I take a step toward the table—I want to get out of here anyway—but Mom's fingers tighten around my elbow and she holds me there. "Whatever you have to say to me, you can say in front of my daughter," Mom says. "You know, she heard what you were saying before."

Mrs. Guthrie licks her lips and takes a big breath in, looks at me for a moment, and then starts talking. "Pamela, I just want to apologize for what I said. I should not have shared what others have been saying, and now I realize I was repeating unfounded rumours and opinions. I am sorry."

Mom smiles. "Thank you, Deirdre, but really you don't owe me an apology at all." Mrs. Guthrie's eyes get wide and she opens her mouth to talk. Before anything comes out, Mom says, "It's Tina you owe an apology to."

Mrs. Guthrie pushes her lips together and then smiles at me. It's a fake smile, even kind of creepy, but I think she is trying. "I'm sorry for doubting you, Tina. I hope you get to play next season."

I don't know what to say, but Mom squeezes my elbow and I know I need to say something. "It's okay," I mumble, and Mrs. Guthrie walks away before anyone can say anything else.

Mom slips her arm around my shoulders and squeezes. "Go swim, have fun," she says, and I go, because being alone in the cold water seems way better than standing here, where I might hear what more adults really think.

CHAPTER 19

Clara Brett Martin
(June 1978)

BASEBALL ISN'T AS GOOD AS HOCKEY, BUT I like it. It's fun to watch too. Last year in Toronto we went to a few Blue Jays games at Exhibition Stadium. It's exciting to see a real baseball team play, but it's more fun to actually play. This year Dad's our coach and J. R. and I are on the same team. It's our first practice.

But then Lindsay shows up. Great. I'm sitting on the bench in the dugout when she comes in. She has a new glove that isn't broken in yet, and it might be the first time I've seen her not wearing a dress. I bend down and retie my laces so I don't stare.

"Hey, Tina," she says. It sounds nice, not snotty.

"Hi," I say back. "I didn't know you played baseball." As soon as I say it I wish I didn't. Did it sound like I was saying she couldn't play baseball? I mean, I'm surprised, but I don't want her to know I think that because she always wears a dress and has pretty hair.

But she doesn't sound insulted when she says, "I haven't before. I mean, I play catch with my brother sometimes, but I finally convinced my dad to let me try it. It took a lot of arguing and he made me promise not to cry if I get hit by the ball, but he finally said yes."

"That's great!" I say, because it really is. Lindsay smiles at me and her eyes are smiling too. It's not a nasty smirk like it was at school.

Dad comes over to the bench and says, "All right kids, let's get started. Go find a spot on the field and I'll hit you some balls."

Dad stands at home plate with a bat that is way too short for him. He calls a name and then tosses a ball into the air, swings the bat with one hand, and hits it out into the infield. I'm on second. When he yells, "TINA!" I get ready and he hits the ball my way. It skips twice off the gravel before I charge to it and scoop it into my glove, turn, and throw it to J. R. at first. I back up toward second to wait for my turn again. Shari plays third. She's really great at catching fast hits in the corner. Lindsay stays in the outfield mostly. She misses a lot of balls, but when she does miss a pop fly and has to run after it, she's really fast.

Dad says, "Last one!" and he hits the ball to J. R. I run over to first to cover the base and he tosses it to me. "All right team, bring it in!" Dad yells, and we run to the bench. I sit beside Shari. She has her red purse on her lap and is rummaging through it. Who brings a purse to a baseball practice? Shari, that's who. She lifts out her Lip Lickers tin, sticks her finger in it, and then runs it over her lips. I can smell the peach. She might not look like a baseball player, but she's got a wicked arm.

Dad stands in front of the bench and smiles at us. "Good first practice, kids! We have one more on Saturday and then a game on Sunday afternoon. Hopefully we'll have uniforms by then, but just in case, try to wear blue T-shirts to the field on Sunday, okay?" Everyone starts to pick up their gear. I watch Lindsay run up to the parking lot and get in a green station wagon.

"Did you know she was playing?" I ask Shari.

"Who? Lindsay?" Shari asks and I nod. "Yeah, I was talking about it and she said it sounded like fun, so I told her she should try. I didn't know if her dad would let her, though."

"I guess he did," I say. "Maybe he'll let her ski with him on the tricky hills next winter."

"Maybe," Shari nods. Up in the parking lot a horn *beep-beep*s. "That's Mom. I'll see you later?"

She puts her purse over her shoulder and starts to hurry away.

"Yeah, come over this afternoon," I call after her. "We can play catch."

She yells, "Okay, I will," as she runs toward the parking lot.

Dad and J. R. are packing the gear bag, fitting the bats in around the bases. Once the bag is packed, Dad stands up and stretches backward. "Take that handle there, J. R.," he says. J. R. takes one handle and Dad takes the other so the bag is lifted between them. I follow them to the parking lot, where they lift the bag into the trunk. The great thing about having Dad as coach is keeping the gear at our place, where we can practice with it all we want. If Shari does come over later, we can hit some balls to each other. Then a thought pops into my head: Maybe I should have invited Lindsay too. That makes me feel a little guilty.

I slide into the back seat of the car and roll down the window. "Hey, Dad?" I say as he sits behind the wheel.

"Yes, Tina?"

"How come I can play baseball? No one said Shari and I can't play because we're girls."

Dad looks at me in the rear-view mirror. "I'm not sure what the difference is, Tina." He backs out of the parking spot, rolls toward the road, looks both ways, and pulls out onto the road.

"Sometimes people get caught up in how things have always been instead of how things should be. Does that make sense?"

"Sorta," I say. I mean, I get what he's saying, but it doesn't make sense to me that hockey has always been for boys. "I'm glad I don't have to fight to play baseball."

"Me too, Tina."

When we pull into the driveway, Julia's red car is parked up by the shed. I jump out and put my bat and glove in the garage. My hockey stick is there, and I'd like to take it out to do some shots, but I know Mom and Dad will want me to go say hello to Julia.

But they're not in the kitchen or the living room. I'm about to give up and head to my room when Dad opens the back door and calls my name. "Come out to the deck and say hello," he says.

I walk through the kitchen to the back deck. Mom and Julia are sitting at the patio table with tall glasses of lemonade in front of them. They're looking out over the field behind our house watching a large flock of birds swoop and rise and float over the field. There must be a hundred or more of them. I don't know how they all know to go the same way.

"Hello," I say.

Julia turns and smiles at me. "Good morning, Tina. How was baseball practice?"

"Good."

"Do you want some lemonade?" Mom asks me.

"Yes please," I say.

"All right, I'll go get you a glass and let you two chat." She stands up and picks up her glass, walking toward the door. "Come on, Rob." She puts her hand on Dad's arm and turns him toward the door as if he's a kid like J. R. or me.

When they've gone through the door, I sit in the chair Mom just left. For a minute Julia doesn't say anything. She's still watching the birds. Is she waiting for me to say something? My hands and feet feel twitchy. I try not to squirm in my seat, but then I notice I'm biting my fingernail, so I sit on my hand. What should I say? I can't think of anything that would sound smart, and the harder I think the more empty my brain gets.

"So you like lots of sports, not just hockey," Julia says before I can figure out something to say first.

"Yes, sports are fun."

"What else do you play?"

"Anything, really. Baseball, tennis, golf. I like swimming too. I want to try downhill skiing sometime."

"That's great," Julia says. "You're quite an athlete." I shrug. I didn't mean to brag.

Thank goodness Mom comes out and hands me a glass of lemonade so I can thank her and not have to say anything to Julia about being good at sports.

Julia takes a sip of her lemonade. "I came to tell you that we have a date for court. We go before the judge August 17. It's a Wednesday."

My stomach flips. It's not a surprise, this is what we were planning, but somehow a date makes it more...real. It's happening.

"Don't be nervous," Julia says as if she read my mind. How do grown-ups do that?

"I'm not," I say, but I am. I'm glad Julia can't hear my heart beating like I hear it, whooshing in my ears.

"Now that we have a date, I'll book some times with your parents to go over the questions with you. We'll do that practice I was talking about, remember?"

I nod.

"You'll see. Once you have some practice and you know what to expect, it'll be easier not to be nervous."

"I'm not nervous," I say, but my voice cracks. She knows I'm lying.

"Tina, your dad is a lawyer, right?" I nod. Why would she ask that? She knows he is. "So you know lots of people your dad has worked with, right?"

I nod again.

"Well, if you think about it, how many of those other lawyers are women?"

Hm. I've been to Dad's office in most of the places he's worked. Some of his offices were fancy, and he had his own room with his own desk and could put pictures on the walls. Other lawyers had their own offices too. Other places, he was in a big room with his own desk up next to someone else's. I try to picture the people I met there and faces flip through my mind: bald heads, moustaches, heavy black glasses, collars and ties, and that one guy who always wore brightly coloured suspenders. There was a woman in Dad's office in Toronto. I used to be scared of her because one of Dad's friends calling her a nasty word, but she was always nice to me. She used to bring in Smarties when she knew J. R. and I were going to be there. A box each, we didn't even have to share.

"One? Maybe a couple more I can't remember."

Julia nods. "When I went to law school there weren't many women. No one said I couldn't go to school because I was a girl, but there were very few of us. My class had eighty-seven students and there were only six women. Think about it."

I think of my class at school. There are twenty-six of us: fifteen girls and eleven boys.

"So even though we were allowed in the class, there were so very few of us. I kind of know what it's like to be in a small group fighting to be included."

"I'm not sure what that means."

Julia pauses to think about it. "Where did you get dressed for hockey?" she asks me.

"I got dressed at home and put my skates on at the rink."

134

"And why didn't you get dressed at the rink?"

Dumb question. "Because the boys were using the dressing room."

"Right. And why isn't there a girls' dressing room?"

Geez, she's supposed to be a smart lawyer. "Because it's just me. Why would they have a dressing room for just one girl?"

Oh. When I hear my words, what she's trying to tell me starts to make sense.

"So, it's like you don't matter. No one thinks about what you need to feel welcome, or what might make other girls feel more welcome. You know, there was a time when women were not allowed to go to law school. Being a lawyer was considered a job for men only."

"Like playing hockey is for boys," I whisper.

"Exactly. Almost one hundred years ago a woman named Clara Brett Martin lived in Toronto. She thought, 'Wait a minute, what if I want to be a lawyer?' I'm sure she had a lot of people who were against her going to law school and a lot of people who made it difficult. But she did and she became the first female lawyer in Canada. And then there were a few more and a few more women. They pushed and worked and showed people that women can be lawyers just like men." She stops talking and looks at me. She smiles. "And so now, I can be a lawyer."

"It's still not fair, though. You just said there were only six girls in your class."

"No, things aren't equal yet, but it's moving that way. We still have to keep trying to make things equitable, or fair. But soon girls will be able to register for hockey without going to court, just like I got to go to law school."

"And there'll be a girls' dressing room?"

I didn't mean to be funny, but Julia laughs. "Yes, I bet there will be."

CHAPTER 20

Just Tell the Truth
(June 1978)

THE LAST DAY OF SCHOOL IS ALWAYS FUN. We never do any work. Mom packed some cookies for me to take for our class party and it takes two hands to carry the container to school. I have to be careful to keep it even so they don't tip together and mess up the icing.

Shari is carrying a large paper bag. "What are you bringing?" I ask her.

"Brownies," Shari says with a smile. Her mom makes good brownies. Mom puts nuts in hers and it's like finding a hard rock when you're chewing something soft. Shari's mom never puts nuts in hers. "What are you bringing?"

"Cookies," I say.

"The ones with icing?"

"Yeah," I nod.

"Right on. Those are to the max."

We walk quickly; we left a few minutes later than we should have. "Are you going away this summer?" I ask.

"Just to the cottage on the weekends."

"Will you miss baseball, then?" Shari is our best hitter. Plus, our team isn't very big; if there are a couple of kids missing we may not be able to field a team.

"I don't know, maybe sometimes," Shari says, kind of bummed. "What about you? Are you guys going away?"

Dad says he's too busy to take enough time to go away. "No, probably not."

"When do you have your court thing?"

My stomach still twists a little when I talk about that. "August 17."

"Are you nervous?"

I wish people would stop asking me that. "No," I say, because I want it to be true. Dad told me last night that we are going to meet with Julia this afternoon after school. I don't want to think about it now, though.

We walk into the schoolyard and Lindsay and Kelly run toward us. Someone behind them yells, "HI, TONY!" but I ignore it.

Lindsay turns around and yells, "Shut up, Connor!" I stop walking and stare. Lindsay and Kelly walk over and stand with us.

"Thanks," I say, because I can't think of anything else to say.

Lindsay shrugs as if she didn't do anything, but she did. She stood up for. First baseball and then this? I didn't see that coming. "What did you bring?" she asks.

"Cookies. What about you?"

Lindsay scrunches up her nose. "My mom made me bring cut-up veggies."

She laughs and that makes me laugh.

"I brought cupcakes," Kelly says.

"Good!" Lindsay says, and that makes us laugh more. The bell rings and we have to hurry to get in line.

The day goes fast, and when the teacher says, "Have a good summer!" the class cheers. My backpack is full of papers and books and assignments that I haven't taken home already, so it's really heavy on my back. Shari and I walk home together. She's talking about something that has to do with her summer plans, but I'm too excited to concentrate. The whole summer is ahead of me, lots of time to play tennis and golf and baseball and practice my slap shot. And once I get past the court day, I'll have nothing to worry about other than what to do each day.

At Shari's house, she says, "See you later, Tina!"

"Bye, Shari!" I say and start walking faster. I want to get some shots in before Dad gets home to take me to meet Julia. At home, I dump my bag on my bed—I'll sort out all the papers later—and change into gym shorts and a T-shirt. I get my stick out of the garage and look around until I've found four tennis balls to shoot.

I drop them onto the driveway and use the blade of my stick to gather them back to my feet as they bounce and roll in four different directions. When they stop rolling, I pull one out separately and shoot it into the net. The next one I send to the lower corner and then up to the top corner. The fourth one misses and hits the garage door with a clang.

I'm gathering all the balls when Dad pulls into the driveway. "Hi, Tina! Happy summer vacation!"

"Thanks!" I set the four balls down gently so they don't bounce and roll away.

Dad walks past me toward the door. "I'll be out shortly. Are you ready to go?"

"Yup," I say and hit one tennis ball with a slap shot. It sails between the posts and hits the back of the net.

"Good shot," Dad says, and I set up the next ball, hoping he sees my next shot too. I flip the ball up into the top corner and it bounces inside the net. I look over my shoulder and Dad smiles at me and nods, then opens the door and goes in.

I get in three more turns with the four balls, shooting, gathering, and shooting again before Dad comes out onto the porch. "Your mother says to change out of your play clothes." I look down at my Scooby Doo T-shirt. It's getting too small, and I'm probably too old for it, but it's my favourite.

"Fine," I say, trying not to sound rude. I gather the balls and set them on top of the net, then lay my stick over the top too. I rush into the house and up to my room and put my school clothes back on—nicer shorts and a shirt with buttons and a collar—and run back down the stairs.

Somewhere in the house Mom yells out, "Careful on the stairs!" but I'm already at the bottom.

"Let's go!" I say to Dad, who is standing on the porch.

I open the car door and get in. The seat is hot on my legs, so I shift back and forth so that neither leg is touching it too long. Dad turns the car around and we head to town.

"Where are we meeting her?" I ask.

"At her office," Dad says without looking away from the road.

"Are you going to stay?" I ask and my voice squeaks at the end. Ugh. I sound like a baby.

He looks at me quickly, then back to the road. "I can if you wish," he says. I nod and my stomach feels a little better.

We pull into a parking lot. The building is square

and two storeys tall, with brick walls and two rows of small windows. We head in the front door and a man in a uniform is sitting behind a desk. I follow Dad to the desk, where he says, "We're here to see Julia MacDougall, please."

"Your name, sir?" the man says while he looks in a big book lying open on the desk in front of him.

"Robert Forbes. The appointment may be in my daughter's name, Tina Forbes."

The man runs his finger over the book while he looks. "Ah, here, yes. Ms. MacDougall is in room 103, just down this hall on the left." He waves his hand toward the door and bends it back to show we need to turn right.

"Thank you," Dad says and heads through the door. I have to walk quickly to keep up.

The door to room 103 is ajar. Dad knocks on it without pushing it open and we hear Julia say, "Come in!" So we do.

Julia's office is small and full with a big desk, a few chairs, and a bookcase stuffed with books and binders and loose papers. Her desk is tidy, with only an open file folder, a phone, a mug, a pad of paper, and a pen on top of it. And a rolodex. Dad has a rolodex on his desk at home, too. I like flipping the pages around and seeing all the names and phone numbers in his handwriting. If I spin it really fast, the pages flip quickly together and look like one big circle. I wonder if our number is in hers. One chair is behind the desk, with two in front of it. One of those chairs has a stack of binders on it.

"Well, hello!" Julia says as she closes the file. She sounds almost surprised to see us, even though we had an appointment. "Oh my, I'm sorry, let me move these," she says, and walks to the chair with all the binders on it. She lifts them up and sets them on the floor behind her desk.

"No bother," Dad says.

"Please have a seat," Julia says. She sits in the chair behind the desk and waves for Dad and I to sit in the two in front. I sit on the edge with my hands under my thighs so I don't chew on my fingernails. I don't want her to know I'm nervous.

"How are you?" Julia asks.

I wait for Dad to answer, but they both look at me. "Good," I say. "Today was the last day of school."

"That's great! Summer vacation was always my favourite time of the year." She has a big smile when she says that.

"Me too," I say.

Julia puts the pad of paper over the closed file folder and pulls it closer to her. There's handwriting on the top page. "Tina, I just wanted to go through some questions with you. Now's the time for us to practice what I'll be asking you in court. We'll meet a few times before our court date to make sure you feel comfortable when the real day comes. Sound good?"

"Okay," I say. I want to ask if Dad can stay, but so far he doesn't seem to be going anywhere, and I don't want to sound babyish again.

"Great. Before we start, can I get you a drink of something? Some water? Some pop?" I perk up and look over at Dad. We're not allowed to drink pop very often. He smiles and nods at me.

"Yes, a pop, please," I say.

Julia bends over behind her desk and I hear a door open. She must have a fridge back there. She hands me a can of Coke, then stands up and walks to the bookcase and passes me a glass from the bottom shelf. "Thank you," I remember to say.

I pull the tab and open the Coke, then pour it into the glass, careful not to spill any. The bubbles rise to the top of the glass and I stop pouring, waiting for them to settle down before continuing. While I'm concentrating on not spilling, Dad and Julia are using big legal words and phrases. I tune them out and watch the bubbles pop in the glass as the fizzy top lowers closer to the dark liquid.

"Tina, your job in the case is to demonstrate that you are the one who wants to play hockey, okay? Which is easy, because that's the truth." I nod, but she keeps talking. "See? The questions will be easy to answer because all we want you to do is go up and tell the truth, okay?" I nod again. I get it. "So let's start at the beginning. The judge will start by asking you easy stuff, like your name,

144

address, birthday, school, and grade. You know all that, right?"

"Yes," I say. Easy.

"Right. And we'll probably ask again, just for the record, and to let you settle in. Then we'll start asking about your sports, what you like to play and what teams you've been on. Shall we practice that?" I nod again. "All right. What sports do you play?"

Wait, does she want me to just talk about hockey season? "Like all the time? Or just in the winter when hockey is on?"

"All the time. I want them to know how much you like sports. I know you do a lot, right? Which ones?"

We'd already talked about this on my deck. "Hockey, of course. And baseball and tennis and golf in the summer. And swimming and skating, do they count?"

Julia's right. Once we get into practicing the questions, the whole thing doesn't seem so scary. The questions are easy and I know all the answers. Julia keeps telling me, "Just tell the truth," and that's all I do, really. She doesn't ask any tricky questions.

"What about the other lawyers?" I ask when Julia says we're finished. "Will they try to trick me?"

Julia looks at me for a minute, then says, "I don't think so, Tina. They will be interviewing a lot of adults too. They will ask different questions than I do, but your job is still the same: Just tell the truth. You can do that, right?"

"Yes," I say.

"We'll meet again and go over questions I think they may ask so you have an idea, but I won't know the exact questions they'll ask. There will be questions that we haven't practiced."

"It's okay," I say, and now it really does feel okay. I know I can do this.

"Right, it's okay," Julia says. "All you have to do is...?" She stops talking so I can tell her.

"Just tell the truth," I say, and she smiles.

"Exactly," Dad says. He's smiling too. I almost forgot he was there.

CHAPTER 21

The Vanguard
(July 1978)

THREE LONG CAR-HORN BLASTS BELLOW FROM down the street: my father's signal for "Come home now!" They've probably already called for me a couple of times, but it seems early for supper.

"I gotta go!" I call out to the other kids. We've been playing catch and monkey in the middle and running bases. I taught them that one: two people put their gloves down and run back and forth between them while the other two people throw the ball back and forth, trying to tag the runners out. First runner to get ten bases without being tagged wins. It was fun until Bobby threw the ball way over my head on purpose so the others could get ten bases on their first try. He's a sore loser.

I pull my bike off the grass and get on, holding the left handlebar with my hand in my glove. It's mostly downhill from here, so I don't have to pedal much, just glide. My speed blows sea wind on my face and lifts my curls.

I turn into our driveway and pedal harder to get up the hill. It's not too steep, but I have to be careful to steer around the potholes too. There's a white station wagon parked behind Dad's car. Who could that be? J. R. is sitting on the porch. "Who's here?" I call up to him as I park my bike against his on the side of the house. I run up the porch steps two at a time.

J. R. rolls his eyes. "Just more of your adoring public." I ignore him and swing open the door.

The screen door bangs behind me and I shout "HELLO! I'm HOME!" as I kick off my sneakers. I remember at the last minute to set them neatly on the mat.

"Tina, come into the kitchen, please," Mom calls back.

I go in and there's a man in a suit sitting at the table. He has a mug in his hand—the "World's Best Dad" mug I painted for Dad last year for Father's Day. On the table in front of him is a long, skinny notepad spiral bound at the top. "Hi Tina," he says as if he knows me already. I don't think I've met him before.

"Tina, this is Mr. Fraser. He's a reporter, and he wants to write a story about you for *The Vanguard*."

For a second I wonder what the Yarmouth newspaper would want with me, but then I realize it must be the court case. That's all anyone wants to talk about, except Mom and Dad and J. R. and me—we'd rather talk about almost anything else. J. R. always says it's boring talking about it. It's not boring to me, but it makes me feel a little sick when I talk about it, even though I've already had four meetings with Julia to practice the questions.

"Your mom is right, Tina. I was hoping to talk to you so I can write a story about you and your hockey. How does that sound?"

I look at Mom and she nods. "All right," I say.

"Great! Your mom has already told me some stuff about how you tried to register, and your dad wrote letters to the provincial and federal associations before he filed the human rights complaint." I nod, but I don't remember a lot of that. I mean, I remember when we took my registration in and I know Dad wrote some letters and called some people, but I don't remember who those were. "So I guess I know a lot about the process that you and your family have done, but I want to hear what you think about all of it."

"I just want to play hockey," I say. I think maybe I've said that a million times. But it still feels like only Mom and Dad and now Julia are actually listening to me.

Mr. Fraser nods and smiles and says, "So I understand. And how did you feel when they said you couldn't play?"

I don't know what he wants me to say. How did I feel? "I dunno, I guess I was sad because I was finally ten, and when we lived in Toronto you could play if you were ten. I didn't know they didn't let girls play here." He is still looking at me and nodding, like I should say more. "I mean, I already had my new hockey skates from Christmas and I had the gear and I wanted to play, and I didn't know they would say I couldn't."

"Sounds like you were disappointed," Mr. Fraser says.

I guess disappointed is a better word than sad. "Yeah," I say.

"So your dad filed the complaint, and what have you done since then?"

"Well, I got to play this year. The lawyer talked to the judge and he said I could play in the meantime. And Julia said she hopes we'll have a permanent decision before registration for this season."

"I see," he says. "And how did your hockey season go?"

"Good. I played centre for some games. Our team didn't win lots of games, but we won the consolation final and I had some goals."

"Yeah? That's great!" Mr. Fraser says, but he's writing on his notepad and he sounds like he didn't really hear me. He looks up and asks, "And how were the other kids on your team? Were they friendly? Were they glad you were there?"

"Yeah. I mean, maybe at first they were worried, but I'm a good skater and they saw I could play good and they were glad when I scored goals." I don't tell him about the bad stuff, how they wouldn't pass me the puck very often or how Chris would check me extra hard in practice if Coach Jim wasn't watching. Telling him wouldn't help anything, I've already told all the grown-ups that matter.

"I bet they were. Say, Tina, I saw you have a net out in the driveway." He stops talking, so I nod. I mean, he saw it, so he knows it's true. "Think I could get some pictures of you taking some shots? I'd like to put a picture in this story if it's okay with you and your mom."

I look up at Mom and she raises her eyebrows. I think she means it's up to me. "Okay," I say. "Now?"

"Sure. Now would be great. I think I've got all the information I want, so we can go out and take some pictures and then I can get out of your hair. Smells like your mom is cooking something delicious for supper. I'd hate to be in the way."

So I put my shoes back on and we go outside. J. R. is shooting on the net and Mr. Fraser says, "Hey son, can we let your sister shoot a bit?"

J. R. just looks at him for a minute. Then he turns and stares at me, biting his lip and glaring. Finally he says, "Sure thing," and throws his stick to the side of the driveway. Good thing Dad didn't see him throw it. He goes up the steps two at a time and forgets not to slam the door.

My stick is still across the top of the net from this morning. I grab it down and take a couple of tennis balls. I'm not sure where he wants me to go to shoot. It's like he reads my mind because he says, "Just start anywhere, Tina. I'll move where I need to get some pictures."

His camera is big and black and fancy. While I shoot I can hear the camera click then wind when he runs his thumb over the lever that moves the film forward.

"That's great, Tina, thanks so much," he says after six or seven clicks. "Thank you, Mrs. Forbes," he says, and I see that Mom is out on the porch. I didn't know she came out with us.

"Of course," Mom says. "Call if you have any more questions."

"I will, thank you," Mr. Fraser says, and then he goes to his car. His legs are long, so he takes big steps and he's in the car before I can put my stick back on the net. I watch him drive down the driveway and turn toward town. That was weird. I've never been in the news before. I don't know if I like the idea or not.

CHAPTER 22

Court Date
(August 17, 1978)

I WAKE UP EARLY. THE SUN IS COMING IN MY window. Then I remember, it's August 17. The day we go to court and talk to the judge. I push my sheet back and get the clothes Mom put out for me last night. I wish I could just wear my shorts and a T-shirt, but Mom said we had to look respectable. At least she's not making me wear a dress. I put on my blue pants and white shirt, then socks and my dress shoes from the closet.

Everyone is already in the kitchen. Mom is cooking a big breakfast; the bacon smells so yummy. I sit in my chair at the table across from J. R., who sticks out his tongue at me. He looks funny wearing his suit. His bony wrists are sticking out of the jacket and his tie is crooked.

"J. R., I saw that," Dad says. He is sitting between us. His tie is straight. He pats my shoulder. "How are you feeling, Tina? Nervous?"

I didn't think I would be, because Julia and I did all those practice questions, but suddenly when Dad asks, my stomach is kind of squirmy. "No, I'm good," I lie.

Dad must believe me, because he says, "Great, you'll do fantastic." Mom puts a plate in front of me: eggs, bacon, and hashbrowns. It's like a celebration breakfast. "Eat up. Pamela, sit and eat yours as well. We'll need to leave soon."

"I'm not sure I can eat," Mom says, bringing a plate to the table and sitting across from Dad. "I'm so nervous." She smiles at me. She doesn't look nervous.

"Nothing to be nervous about," Dad says.

"I don't know why I even have to go," J. R. says. "Can't I stay home? They don't want to talk to me, so why do I even have to go waste my whole day in some stupid courtroom?"

"To support your sister," Mom says.

"We've talked about this," Dad says at the same time. "We're not going to discuss it again." He wipes a piece of toast over his plate through the egg yolk and stuffs it in his mouth. He stands up, lifts his plate, and walks to the sink. J. R. sticks his tongue out at me again. I wish he didn't have to go, but I'm kind of glad he will be there. "Hurry up, kids, it's time to go."

"Rob, it's barely eight o'clock, we have lots of time to get there," Mom says.

"I don't want to be late," Dad says. I'm not sure how we could be. Dad said the judge would start at ten and the courthouse is just in town, like five minutes away. And it's not winter, like when I want to make sure we're not late for hockey because of the snow.

But Mom looks at me and says, "Eat up, Tina," so I hurry to eat my potatoes and bacon. I leave the eggs. My stomach is still kind of sick and the runny yolk doesn't look too good all of a sudden. I manage to throw the egg in the garbage when Dad leaves the kitchen and Mom's not looking and I go brush my teeth. Maybe that'll make me feel a bit better.

WHEN WE PULL INTO THE courthouse parking lot we're almost the only car there. I see Julia's car, so she's early too. I don't recognize any of the others. I wonder if the judge is here already. We follow Dad into the courthouse and into the courtroom. I've only seen in the inside of the courtroom from the show *The Rockford Files*. When the private investigator, John Rockford, goes to court, the judge sits on a big wooden stand, and the jury sits in a wooden box. I guess there's no jury in this court, but there's no big wooden stand either, just a wooden desk. I wonder if the judge minds not having a big seat. There are chairs set up in rows on either side of an aisle, behind two tables that are smaller than the judge's wooden desk. In *The Rockford Files* you have to pick a side, like a wedding we went to once. I wonder which side is ours, but then Dad points to some seats near the front, so we all sit there. I'm between Mom and J. R.

Julia comes through a door on the other side of the room. She looks pretty, but also serious, with a suit that has a skirt and a white blouse with a wide collar. I wish my shirt had a collar like that. She walks over to us and her heels *click-click-click* on the floor. "Hi guys," she says and shakes Dad's hand. "I didn't expect you so early, but I'm happy to see you." She looks at me. "Think you're ready, Tina?"

"Yup," I say. I am. I'm glad we practiced the questions.

"So, like we talked about, Tina, your dad is going to go first. Then it'll be your turn. Okay?" I nod. I hear the door we came in swing open with a bang. I turn to see two men walk in. They are dressed in suits like Dad and are carrying briefcases. They walk in fast, past us, to the table on the other side of the aisle.

"That's Mr. Rose and Mr. Sloane, the lawyers representing the Yarmouth Minor Hockey Association," Julia whispers to me. I wonder if it's a secret that we know who they are. I mean, it shouldn't be, because they have to ask me the other questions, Julia told me that, but I don't know why else Julia would be whispering. "All right, I must excuse myself to go get ready. Please make yourself comfortable. I'm sure we'll start right on time," Julia says. She smiles at all of us and then turns and *click-click-click*s back to the table in front of our chairs. I wish she could sit with us. Mr. Rose walks over to her and puts his hand out. She shakes it and they say things I can't quite hear.

People come in and sit behind us, on our side and on the other side of the aisle. I recognize some people from the rink and some people from around town. Mr. Fraser comes in carrying his notepad. After a bit I get tired of looking back every time the door bangs open, so I just watch the long hand on my watch go around until it's almost ten o'clock.

The door that Julia came through opens and the judge comes in. He's younger than I thought he'd be; he's not bald and his hair is black, not white. He has a big moustache and he's smiling when he sits down. "It is ten o'clock by my watch, and if everyone is agreeable, perhaps we might begin the proceedings." When the judge says this, everyone else stops talking. The lawyers at the front of the room sit in their chairs and look up at him. The room is quiet. "For those who don't know me, my name is Judge R. E. Kimberly. I am a member of the Provincial Court of Nova Scotia...." The judge says some words I understand, like "Human Rights Act" and "complaint," and lots I don't, until: "by Mr. Robert Forbes, who is a barrister, on behalf of his daughter, Tina Forbes, a minor, and he is the complainant in this matter." That's us. "The respondent is the Yarmouth Minor Hockey Association." When he says that, I think of Mr. Hickman at the bank, even though Dad says he is only one person who is part of the hockey association. The judge is still talking, but it's hard to follow what he says with all the legal words. I sneak a look at Dad on the other side of J. R. He's looking at the judge and nodding. His face is serious, his eyebrows pointing down like when he's concentrating at his desk. Mom, on the other side of me, is watching the judge and concentrating too. I look at J. R. He's picking fluff off his pants. When he looks up and sees me watching him, he sticks out his tongue at me. I stick mine back out at him.

The judge stops talking for a minute and the lawyers stand up and they all say, "Agreed." I'm not sure what they agreed to. For a bit the judge and the lawyers keep talking. I try to listen, I really do, but it's really boring. I guess I expected this to be a bit more exciting.

But then the judge says, "Mr. Forbes?"

Dad stands up beside J. R. and says, "I concur." I'm not sure what he's agreeing with.

Beside Julia her partner, Mr. Houghman, stands up. He's a nice man. He worked with us once when we were practicing the questions, but he said Julia could ask me in court. Mr. Houghman says, "Your honour,"—that's the judge—"I am acting for Mr. Forbes and his daughter as well as for the Human Rights Commission."

Judge Kimberly says, "Oh, I see. So Mr. Forbes is interested, but at least not active."

Huh?

Mr. Houghman says, "No, no, not as a solicitor or as a barrister."

I remember now, how Mr. Houghman and Dad agreed it would be better if he was in court just as my dad and the complainant, not as a lawyer. Dad said, "They already say I'm doing this to make a name for myself, it would be better if I'm not involved at all," and Mr. Houghman agreed. That's why Julia is asking me the questions and not Dad, even though he's a lawyer too.

The judge and the lawyers keep talking at the front and I count the people in the courthouse (forty-seven) and the windows (thirteen). Then I try to remember all the players on the Sabres by their position, first the forwards, then the defence, then the goalie and the backup goalie. When I remember as many of them as I can, I start remembering the New York Rangers. I'm trying to think of their last defenceman when I hear Mr. Houghman say, "Yes, I call Robert Forbes."

CHAPTER 23

Dad, Not Lawyer
(August 17, 1978)

D AD STANDS BESIDE ME AND WALKS OVER TO a chair by the judge's desk. A man in uniform comes and holds a Bible in front of Dad. Dad puts his hand on it and the man mumbles something I can't hear, then Dad says, "I do" and sits.

Mr. Houghman is standing by his table. I can't see his face, but Dad smiles at him. "Mr. Forbes, would you state your full name for the record?" Seems strange that they use his name to ask him to say his name.

Dad says, "Robert Charles Forbes."

"Where do you reside?"

"In Hebron, Yarmouth County, Nova Scotia." Mr. Houghman asks Dad lots of the questions Julia and I practiced, though instead of asking about school, he asks about his job and where he works now and where he used to work. It takes some time, because Dad has had a lot of jobs and we've moved a lot for him to work in different places.

"Do you have any children besides Tina?" Mr. Houghman asks.

"Yes, I have one other. Robert Charles Forbes the Second."

I snicker a bit and J. R. elbows me in the ribs. It sounds silly to hear J. R.'s full name.

Mr. Houghman holds up some papers and shows them to Dad. "Would you identify these papers, Exhibit D-1, then, please?"

Dad takes the papers and looks at them for a second, then says, "Exhibit D-1 is a complaint under the Human Rights Act, dated at Digby, December thirteenth, 1977, and it is signed by me." He hands the papers back to Mr. Houghman, who gives them to the man in the uniform who held the Bible out for Dad.

Mr. Houghman walks back in front of Dad again. He says, "Could you please outline the events that led you to laying this complaint that your daughter was discriminated against?"

Dad looks at me and winks, then looks back at Mr. Houghman and says, "Well it all started on the twenty-fourth of September, 1977. It was registration day for Yarmouth Minor Hockey. I went down to the Bank of Nova Scotia on Main Street to register both of my children, Tina and Robert." I snicker again; I can't help it. This time Mom shushes me. Dad keeps telling Mr. Houghman about how he filled out the forms and gave them to Mr. Hickman behind the table and how Mr. Hickman asked if I was a girl because my name was Tina.

Mr. Houghman looked up from his paper and asks Dad, "Were you told then that your daughter could not register for Minor Hockey?"

"Yes," Dad says. His voice is strong and clear.

"And did Mr. Hickman indicate to you any reason?"

Before Dad can answer, Mr. Rose says, "Well, he just said it."

Mr. Houghman looks at Mr. Rose and tries to smile, I think. His face kind of winces. "What were you led to believe was the reason your daughter couldn't register?"

Dad says, "She was a girl."

Mr. Rose stands up and interrupts, "That is not what he said, apparently...." He goes on to argue about who said what, the provincial or the federal hockey people, and no one says anything to him about interrupting. Why is he arguing about who said I couldn't play? The point is, someone said it.

The judge waves his hand and Mr. Rose stops talking. "That is easily resolved by simply asking Mr.

Forbes what his understanding was," Judge Kimberly says.

Dad nods. "I can say that my understanding at that point in time was that my daughter was not permitted to register for Minor Hockey in the Town of Yarmouth because the Nova Scotia Minor Hockey Council and the CAHA forbid girls from playing."

Mr. Houghman asks Dad about all the people he wrote to and called to try and get them to change their minds. Dad is good at remembering dates and names, and he answers the questions easily. He's not nervous, even though I don't think he practiced answering the questions with Mr. Houghman as much as I practiced with Julia. I guess he's just used to courtroom questions.

Mr. Rose keeps interrupting, though. It seems like he's splitting hairs—that's what Mom calls it when J. R. and I are fighting about something and we won't admit we're saying the same thing only a little bit differently. One time Mr. Rose even stands up and slams his hands down on the desk and says, "Now, what good is that? What has Mr. Cooper got to do with it? He may have received a letter from the Queen of England, and are we going to admit that too?" What does the Queen of England have to do with any of this, is my question, but Mr. Houghman doesn't ask that; he just says something about evidence. This would go a lot faster if Mr. Rose would stop interrupting.

Mr. Houghman starts asking Dad about starting a girls' league. I liked that idea when we talked about it, but the problem is there aren't enough girls. You need fifteen skaters on a team plus a goalie, and some teams two goalies. Dad said that before we moved here they only got six girls to come out and play. That's not even one full team. Who would we play against?

Mr. Houghman walks back to his desk and lays his papers down. "Those are all my questions, unless you have anything else you feel you should add, Mr. Forbes?"

Dad smiles and says, "No."

"Thank you," Mr. Houghman says and sits down.

Mr. Rose stands up. He's asking Dad about following rules, all the rules for hockey. I'm not sure what the rules have to do with it; an offside is the same for a girl or a boy. When I played this year, I didn't have different rules. Then he says something about Canadian regulations, but not in a game. He must mean about following rules that say girls can't play.

"What are you after in this whole matter?" Mr. Rose asks Dad.

"I want my daughter to play hockey," Dad says.

"You want your daughter to play hockey whether it is integrated with males or not?" Mr. Houghman asks Dad.

Dad doesn't want me to play; I want to play. But Dad doesn't say that, he says, "It matters not."

"You would be satisfied, then, if there were a girls' hockey team consisting of five other girls, and she could play hockey with the girls?" Mr. Houghman says. He must not have been listening when they talked about how many skaters you need on a team. Maybe they should have practiced their questions more, and Dad could have told him you need more than five girls. That's not even enough to change lines!

"Definitely," Dad says. He doesn't argue that we need more than one line to make a team.

"And you are not after her to play with boys necessarily?"

"Not necessarily, no." I don't care if I play with girls or boys. I guess that's what Mr. Houghman and Dad are trying to show the judge.

"Now, theoretically, if there had been a girls' league, that was all that you were after?"

"Definitely," Dad says again.

"Did you make that clear to anybody?"

"I made it as clear as I could make it. I tried to register her with the boys because that was all there was. There's no big deal, the girls can just go out and play with the boys. When they get their helmets on they all look alike. They're all hockey players."

Mr. Rose asks Dad questions, but the way he asks is different from Mr. Houghman. He sounds like he's trying to trick Dad into saying something, like when Mom tricks J. R. or me into admitting we took the last cookie or cleaned our rooms by putting all of our mess in the closet or under the bed. He asks Dad about dressing rooms, and Dad tells him that I get dressed at home. He asks Dad about how bad I'd feel if I couldn't play on the rep team, even if I was good enough, and Dad says it's worse not to play at all. That's true. I just want to play on any team. With all his questions, he doesn't trick Dad once. Dad's too good. He even asks Dad about the news following the story. I glance back at Mr. Fraser, but Mr. Fraser is focused on what Dad is saying and doesn't see me looking.

"Did you have any correspondence or any conversations with anybody outside of the province that knew about it?" Mr. Rose asks. Mr. Fraser wrote the article for *The Vanguard* in Yarmouth, but maybe he told people in other provinces about me.

"Oh, yes," Dad says. He did? I guess I should have known that, but I didn't really think about it much. Good thing, too, because thinking about it makes my stomach churn just a bit.

"And you knew that it was becoming a cause of celebrity for you. What if I suggest you were enjoying it?"

I can't see Mr. Rose's face, but Dad looks mad now, like when I've done something wrong and he tells me I'm in trouble. "I suggest to you that you are wrong," he says in his angry voice. I know some people think Dad is trying to get famous with all this. It's not true, he just wants me to be able to play hockey.

I don't like listening to Mr. Rose. I don't like that he makes Dad mad. So I stop listening. I poke J. R. in the arm and leg until he shoves me back and Mom frowns at both of us. I wish I had brought some paper to draw on.

After a long time, Mr. Rose sits down and Mr. Houghman stands back up. I didn't know he'd get another turn to ask questions, but Dad smiles and it's probably a good thing that he can talk to Mr. Houghman again instead of finishing with Mr. Rose trying to trick him. Mr. Houghman asks Dad some questions and Dad is smiling again.

Dad looks at me and says, "It would have been very easy for me as the parent of a ten-year-old daughter to say to her, 'Sorry, but the powers that be have told me that you cannot play, and there is nothing I can do about it.' She didn't know about the Human Rights Act. She had no idea that she had the right to appeal this to a court or to a special committee. I advised her of that, and it would have been very easy for me to just back off. I have been called a young buck lawyer trying to make a name for myself. I was asked to do a radio interview, a television interview, and many more. On most occasions I have declined because I don't want the publicity." He stops and smiles at me. "I just want my daughter to be able to play hockey. It is that simple."

"Thank you, Mr. Forbes." Mr. Houghman turns and smiles at me too, then looks back at the judge and says, "Those are all my questions, your honour."

The judge nods and Dad comes back to sit beside J. R. He reaches over and squeezes my hand.

"Are there other witnesses you will call?" the judge asks.

Mr. Houghman is still standing by his table. "Yes, we are prepared to proceed with Tina Forbes. At this point, though, perhaps we could have a break?"

The judge looks at his wrist. "Well, it is twelve thirty. I think if Counsel wants to continue, it might be wise to adjourn for lunch first."

The lawyers are nodding.

Judge Kimberly says, "We will adjourn the inquiry until two o'clock. Thank you." He stands up and walks out of the room.

MOM PACKED SANDWICHES and carrot sticks with ranch dressing. She hands a sandwich to me and I unwrap the wax paper around it. It's peanut butter and jelly, my favourite. Dad has a chicken sandwich. The lettuce is sticking out of the bread and a bit of mayo sticks to his lips when he takes his first bite.

"This is all very interesting," Mom says. It's not polite to argue, so I don't say anything. "You did very well, Rob."

Dad smiles at her. "I did all right."

"Mr. Rose was trying to trick you," I say.

168

Dad puts his hand on my head and messes up my hair. I put my sandwich down and smooth it out again. It's hard to look respectable with messy hair. "It's not really tricking, Tina. He's trying to make the judge see things from his perspective instead of mine."

"Will he try to trick me too?"

"No. Remember, just answer the questions with the truth, and he can't make you say anything wrong." I remember, and I'll tell the truth, but it still makes me nervous that Mr. Rose will try to make me say something the wrong way and tell the wrong perspective. "Julia will be there to ask more questions if he does mix things up. That's called a rebuttal. Remember that Mr. Houghman asked me more questions at the end?"

That's right. "Yeah, I remember," I say.

"That was to make sure the judge heard our perspective the way we meant it. Don't worry, just tell the truth."

Just tell the truth. I can do that. I take another bite of my sandwich and try to remember the questions Julia and I practiced in her office. There weren't all these people in her office, though. And there wasn't Mr. Rose. Julia did try to guess some of the questions he might ask, but she asked them in her nice voice, not in the tricky, angry voice Mr. Rose used when he asked Dad all those questions. Suddenly my sandwich doesn't taste all that great. I fold the wax paper around what's left.

"You should eat, Tina," Mom says. Of course she noticed me wrapping it back up.

"I'm not hungry," I say, careful not to talk back.

Dad takes my sandwich from me. He unwraps it and takes a big bite. "Don't force her, Pamela, she's fine," he says with his mouthful. "Perhaps she'd prefer some of those cookies you're hiding in that bag?"

"Robert, I was keeping those for when the children were done their lunch!" Mom says, but she's just pretending to be mad. She pulls a brown bag out and gives me a chocolate chip cookie. I only take a small bite, because my stomach is still swirling, but it tastes good.

I manage to eat two cookies, taking small bites, before Dad says, "Let's take a walk and get some fresh air." Mom packs up the garbage from our lunch and tosses it in the garbage can. Dad says we can leave our things there, that no one will bother them, and we walk outside. The sun is warm and the air smells like salt water. The tide must be in. J. R. and I run ahead of Mom and Dad. It feels good to move and stretch and run, and for a bit I try not to think about it being my turn to answer the questions in the courtroom.

CHAPTER 24

What's an Oath?
(August 17, 1978)

M Y WATCH SHOWS EXACTLY TWO O'CLOCK when the judge returns and sits behind his desk. Julia stands up and says, "I call Tina Forbes." That means it's my turn to go sit in the chair beside the judge. The man in the uniform comes over with the Bible, and I remember how Dad stood by the chair before sitting down, so I stand still.

The judge says, "Tina, sit down for a moment. I want to ask you some questions before swearing you in." Julia didn't say anything about the judge asking me questions, but he's smiling at me and his voice is nice, so maybe it won't be too bad. I sit down with my hands under my thighs so I don't fidget or bite my nails. I look out at Mom and Dad and J. R., who gives me a thumbs up.

"First of all, tell me your name," the judge says, even though he knows it.

"Tina Marie Forbes," I say. Easy-peasy.

"And what is your address?"

"Hebron." I don't have a long address; we're the only Forbeses in Hebron.

"And how old are you?"

Another easy one—these were all the questions Julia was going to ask me. This is not so bad. "Eleven."

"Your birthday?"

"March 6."

"Nineteen...?"

For a minute I think he thought I said nineteen instead of six, even though they don't sound at all alike, but then I realize he's asking me what year. Hmm. Nineteen sixty-what? Seven. That's right. "Seven," I say.

"Sixty-seven?"

Oops. "Yes."

The judge asks more of the questions Julia and I practiced, about school and church and stuff. I just tell the truth, and it's not too bad.

"If I asked you what it means to be honest, would you be able to answer that question, do you think?" he asks. But before I can answer, he keeps talking. "It is not an easy question. Do you know what it means to be honest?

It's not that hard. "Not to lie."

"Do you know what it means not to cheat?"

Well, there's different cheating, depending on whether you're in school or playing sports. I start to say, "Don't copy or—"

He must have meant in school, because he asks another question before I can talk about cheating at baseball or hockey or golf. "Do you know what it means to tell the truth?"

"Don't lie, and tell the thing that really happened."

"If I ask you what an oath is, do you know what that word means?"

I've heard it before, maybe when Dad was talking about work? But I don't remember exactly what it means. It's not a word Julia and I talked about or practiced. "No," I say. I hope I'm still allowed to answer all of Julia's questions.

"Okay," the judge says. "Do you know what it means to swear to tell the truth? Do you know what that means?"

Yeah, Dad had to swear to tell the truth before he answered the questions. "To tell the truth," I say.

"Do you know what it means to promise to tell the truth?"

Same thing. "To tell the truth."

"And if you promise to tell the truth and didn't tell the truth, is that a good thing or a bad thing?"

"Bad." Obviously.

"Why?"

"Because you said you would and you didn't."

The judge smiles and me and nods, so I guess I answered the questions okay.

"I think she is quite capable of being sworn," he says. "Will you stand up, Tina?" I stand up and the man in the uniform comes over with the Bible. "Place your right hand on the Bible," the judge says, so I think for a minute to make sure I have the right hand and put it on the Bible. The judge says, "Do you swear, or promise—in this particular context it means the same thing—in the matter of this inquiry, to tell the truth, the whole truth, and nothing but the truth, so help you God?"

Julia told me he'd ask this and that I was to say yes. She smiles when I say it.

"Okay," the judge says, "sit down, Tina. The lawyers will ask you questions, so speak up so everyone can hear your answers." Julia's office was small enough that I didn't have to talk very loudly for everyone to hear me.

CHAPTER 25

Tina's Shot
(August 17, 1978)

JULIA STANDS UP AND SMILES AT ME. I'M GLAD she gets to go first. She told me before that when she stands up I should take a deep breath, so I breathe in as far as I can and let it go slowly like we practiced. That makes my heart feel a little more quiet. But then when I'm watching Julia walk toward me I notice Chris sitting in the back row beside his mom. What is he doing here? I'm glad you're not allowed to talk in a courtroom, because I bet he'd shout something nasty at me up here if he could. I look back at Julia and take another breath and try to forget Chris sitting back there.

"Will you state your full name for the record?" she asks, even though the judge already asked that and I already said it and everyone knows what my name is anyway.

Julia asks all the easy questions we practiced about my address and going to school, even though the judge already asked them too. She asks about what sports I like to play and I tell her and everyone else as loudly as I can without shouting: "Baseball, swimming, hockey on the ponds, skating, golfing." She asks about the hockey equipment I got for Christmas and I tell them about my skates, gloves, pads, stick, and puck.

"Do you want to play hockey quite badly? Do you like hockey?" she asks.

"Yes."

"Now, what can you tell us about playing hockey? Who would you like to play hockey with? Have you any preference?"

When we practiced, Julia said to answer this question with a simple answer, not too much information about rinks and teams and jerseys. "No, I don't really care. I just want to play hockey."

"You just want to play hockey?" she asks again.

"Yes," I say. Just tell the truth.

"That is all my questions," Julia says and winks at me.

Phew, that wasn't so hard. I stand up and start to head back to my seat, careful not to look over toward

Chris, but the judge says, "Come back a minute now, Tina, and sit down." Oh yeah. I forgot about Mr. Rose's turn.

MR. ROSE STANDS UP and walks a bit closer to me. He smiles. I remember to take the deep breath Julia and I practiced. But I think I need another—in... out....

"Tina, the baseball team that you play on is coached by your dad, eh?" he asks.

I don't know why he's talking about baseball; we're here to talk about hockey. "Yes," I say anyway.

"And how many other girls play with you on that team?"

I think about Shari, carrying her purse to the field, and Lindsay with her brand new glove. "Just two."

"Just two. And when you take golf lessons, who do you take golf lessons from?"

"Mrs. Judge."

"From a lady?"

I try not to frown. Of course it's a lady; her name is Mrs. Judge. "Yes," I say.

"Do you remember when your dad made this application for you to play hockey here?"

A picture of Mr. Hickman giving my application back to Dad pops into my head. "Yes," I say.

"In Toronto when you and your dad and your mom, I suppose, talked about you coming to Yarmouth, did you know that there was a rink here?"

"Yes."

"And would you rather play hockey with girls than with boys?"

"It doesn't matter. I just want to play hockey." Why is that so hard for everyone to believe?

Mr. Rose asked some questions about J. R. and me going to public skating on Sundays and I answer them. They're easy, easier than the questions Julia and I practiced. Then he turns to the judge and says "Thank you," but I don't know what he's thanking him for. I'm the one who answered his questions.

Judge Kimberly looks at me then and smiles. He says, "Thank you very much, Tina." That means I can go back to my seat with Mom and Dad and J. R.

And just like that I'm done. That wasn't so bad after all.

MOM IS NEXT. Julia calls her name and Mom goes up to the chair. She puts her hand on the Bible and says "I do" when they ask her about telling the truth. She didn't have to talk about what telling the truth means, like I did. I guess it's because she's a grown-up and should know about that already.

Julia asks Mom about her name and address and when we moved here. They talk about Mom coaching at the rink. Julia asks her about all my sports and Mom tells her about how I played baseball and did swimming lessons and skating and gymnastics in Toronto and Winnipeg before we came here.

"With regard to her playing hockey, has she expressed her feelings about playing hockey in Yarmouth since your family relocated here?"

"Yes, and of course she had expressed her feelings about playing hockey in Toronto. We just obviously assumed too much, thinking that she would be allowed to play. She was really up for playing hockey and rather disappointed when she couldn't."

Julia looks at her paper and then looks back up and Mom and asks, "Has she ever expressed to you how she feels about playing or who she wishes to play with, if anyone in particular?"

"Tina doesn't really care." I really don't. "She just wants to play hockey. She doesn't care whether it is with boys or girls or men or women. She just wants to go out and play hockey and enjoy herself and have a good time." Though playing with kids would be more fun than playing with grown-ups.

Julia says, "You are quite familiar with her skating ability?"

"With hers, yes." Mom says.

"How would you describe it?"

Mom smiles. "I would say that she is quite a good skater." Hearing Mom say that makes me feel warm all over. "She is a strong skater. She is well coordinated. She is fast and has a good knowledge of skating, such as backward skating, crosscuts, that sort of thing. She is well versed in skating."

"What is the most important part of being a good hockey player? What makes a good hockey player?"

"I would say skating ability."

Julia is finished. She sits behind her table beside Mr. Houghman and Mr. Rose stands up.

Mr. Rose asks Mom about the gymnasts in the Commonwealth Games. Why does he keep asking questions about stuff other than hockey? I don't get it. But then he starts talking about girls' sports and girls' golf teams and girls' gymnastics, and I understand. He's trying to prove that girls should only play with girls. But there's no girls' hockey team here!

"When you came to a small town, you and your husband felt that your daughter was being discriminated against, why? Because there wasn't a girls' team, or because she wasn't allowed to play with the boys?" Mr. Rose asks.

Mom looks right at Mr. Rose with a serious face. "She wanted to play hockey. There was no girls' team and we felt that if she wanted to play hockey badly enough, she should be allowed to play on a boys' team. And I personally feel that she has the right to play."

"Does your girl belong to Brownies?"

"She is a Girl Guide."

"What would you think of a boy asking to join Girl Guides?" This question makes me think of J. R. flying up to Guides and I giggle. I think maybe he's thinking the same thing, because I catch him smiling a little.

"Well, it is fine, I guess, if they want to join Girl Guides." I'm still picturing J. R. in a Girl Guide uniform. I cover my mouth so no one hears my giggle and J. R. elbows me to be quiet.

"What would you think if your daughter wanted to join Scouts?"

"If she truly wanted to join Scouts and did not want to belong to Girl Guides, I would back her." Mom's chin rises up a little. It's her "Go ahead, try me" look. J. R. and I never dare try it.

"You know there are no girls in Boy Scouts."

"Yes," Mom says.

"Do you think that is wrong?"

"No, I don't think it's wrong. I am just saying that if that were what my daughter wanted, I would try to help." But I don't want to be in Boy Scouts. This would be over much faster if Mr. Rose would just stay on topic.

"Would you try to talk her out of it? Let's be honest."

Mom looks at me. "Probably. Like I tried to talk her out of hockey." I remember when Dad told me about discrimination and the Human Rights Act and Mom tried to convince me that figure skating and pond hockey would be enough. But when I said I still wanted to play, she said, "What's next?" and Dad made the complaint.

Mr. Rose is finished with Mom and Julia and Mr. Houghman do not have to ask more questions to get the judge to see the right perspective. Mom comes and sits beside me and squeezes my hand. I squeeze back.

CHAPTER 26

The Tina Forbes Problem
(August 17, 1978)

MR. ROSE SAYS A NAME AND I HEAR A CHAIR scrape the floor behind me. A man is walking to the front. He has a blue suit on that is baggy and kind of wrinkled. He's not wearing a tie; instead, his collar is open a few buttons. He sits down and they start asking questions. The questions are all about money and numbers, and I close my eyes for just a second because I can't listen to any more boring talk.

Mom nudges me and I open my eyes. I think I fell asleep. I rub my eyes to make them open wider and try to listen to the man at the front. It's still the guy with the wrinkly jacket.

"And I think you have told us that until this year you have never had a young lady apply to join?" Mr. Rose asks.

"No," the man says. His voice laughs a little when he says it. I don't know what's so funny.

"What I really want to know is: what was the reasoning behind the refusal of Tina Forbes registering to play hockey?" Mr. Rose leans forward over his desk when he says that, putting his hands on the desk.

"It was against the rules of the Nova Scotia Minor Hockey Council. We weren't permitted to register girls. If we registered a girl, Yarmouth Minor Hockey could be suspended from the council." He's not laughing anymore. It sounds like he's mad, like he's spitting the words out.

"What would that do to minor hockey in Yarmouth?" Mr. Rose asks.

"It would have a detrimental effect on the whole organization, but probably it would do more harm to the boys. We are not involved strictly with boys chasing a puck around the ice; we are involved in other things that broaden the boys' scope. Some of our boys have never been out of Yarmouth before they start travelling with the hockey team. They get to see where other teams live and interact with the families that they billet with and so on. If Yarmouth Minor Hockey were suspended, it would probably be worse for the boys than anybody else."

But that's not fair. I didn't ask to go on a travel team and I didn't ask them to stop a travel team from going anywhere. I just wanted to play hockey on a house league team, and we told them that. If I stood up now and said that, I wonder if they would listen, if they would hear that this guy in his wrinkly suit isn't telling the whole truth the way he said he would. But I don't stand up, because it's not my turn. I'm supposed to just sit quietly and listen. I make my fists again and push them into my thighs to keep myself in my seat. My eyes water. Maybe because my fists kind of hurt or maybe something else.

Mr. Houghman stands up and walks toward the man. The first thing he asks is if there even is a travel team for kids my age that I could play on if I wanted to, and the wrinkly-suit man has to admit there isn't. Good. I'm glad Mr. Houghman was paying attention and caught him not telling the whole truth.

Mr. Houghman asks, "Have any German children ever registered for minor hockey in Yarmouth?"

"Not that I'm aware of. Perhaps there could be."

"Any Ukrainian children?"

"No."

"Is it a custom in Yarmouth, then, that you don't allow German or Ukrainian children to play hockey?"

"Not that I am aware of."

"Does Yarmouth Minor Hockey prevent Catholic children from playing in the hockey system?"

"No."

"Protestant children?" I get it. He's talking about discrimination.

"No."

"Jewish children?"

"No."

"Any discrimination on religion at all?" I knew it!

"Not that I know of."

"What about the basis of race, is there any preference?

"None whatsoever." That's true. Carl on my team has brown skin. He's allowed to play without going to court.

"But Yarmouth Minor Hockey Association wouldn't let Tina Forbes play because she's a girl?"

The wrinkly-suit man pushes himself up a bit in his chair then settles down again. He looks fidgety. "Because the rules say that boys play." That's not what Mr. Houghman asked him, though.

"It was because she was a girl, then?"

"Well, I suppose." Ha! Mr. Houghman got him to admit it!

"Do you think girls should be allowed to play with boys? Do you personally see anything wrong with that?" Mr. Houghman asks.

"I wouldn't let my daughters play at that age with boys. I think there are certain things that you know are right and certain things that are wrong."

I think of Lindsay and her dad not letting her

ski down the bigger hills and I'm sad for this man's daughters. Why shouldn't they play any sport if they want to? What else do they want to do that he doesn't let them? Are they allowed to play baseball? Or what about the math club at school—can they do that?

While I'm wondering what else his daughters might miss out on, they keep talking about meetings and rules and exhibits and I stop paying attention. The judge and Mr. Rose and even Mr. Houghman do some more talking, and then wrinkly-suit man goes back to his seat. When he walks past me he looks right at me. His eyebrows are bushy and they come together when he frowns at me. His lips are thin and white under his fuzzy moustache. I try not to look away, but his staring makes my stomach jump a bit and I look down at my hands. I wish people weren't so angry over me wanting to play hockey.

Mr. Rose says, "I call Pete Murray to the stand."

I turn and see a very skinny and tall man stand up. Mr. Murray? What? That's Mr. Murray, Chris's father! So all this time Chris was bugging me about playing hockey, his dad was one of the people who didn't want me to play.

Mr. Murray walks up to the front and does the swearing in part with the Bible then sits down. He has hair around the sides of his head, but not on top, so he grew one side long and brushed it over. But the part he brushed over isn't staying down; it's sticking up a bit, like it's windy in here. While he talks to

Mr. Rose, he nods his head and the long windy parts bounce. I have to try really hard not to laugh.

Mr. Rose says, "Were you familiar with this Tina Forbes problem?" Mr. Murray nods and his long hairs flop back and forth over his head. I watch the hairs instead of thinking about how Mr. Rose just called me a problem.

After Mr. Rose sits down, Mr. Houghman gets up and asks more questions. He gets Mr. Murray to admit he doesn't think it's right for girls to play either. I wish someone would ask *why* these men think it isn't right for girls to play with boys.

Judge Kimberly makes sure all the questions are done, and then Mr. Murray stands up and walks back to the seats. He doesn't look at me, he just stares forward, so I watch him go down the aisle behind me. He sits beside Chris and then pats Chris on the head. And then Chris looks right at me. I get ready to stick my tongue out at him if he makes a nasty face, but he doesn't. He looks at me a minute and then shrugs one shoulder up and does a half smile. If he weren't Chris Murray, I would think maybe he meant he was sorry. Mom bumps me with her elbow because I'm staring and I turn back to face the front and don't stick out my tongue.

Judge Kimberly, Mr. Rose, and Mr. Houghman talk about being done for the day. They agree to come back at nine tomorrow, and finally the judge says, "Adjourned."

CHAPTER 27

What Chris Said
(August 17, 1978)

WE START TO WALK OUT OF THE COURTHOUSE together, but people keep stopping Dad to talk to him. At first we stop too and stand and wait for them to stop chatting, but the third time someone wants to speak to him, Dad says to Mom, "Pamela, why don't you take the children to the car?"

Mom nods and says, "Let's go."

We walk a little bit, and when we go around to the side of the building there's a bright flash. It's Mr. Fraser taking a picture of Chris. I stop and J. R. bumps into the back of me.

"Move it!" he says, but I don't move. Mr. Fraser talks to Chris and writes in his notebook like when he asked me all those questions. Of all the people here today, why does Mr. Fraser have to talk to Chris? He's just going lie like he always does and say I can't skate or shoot and I'm just a girl. Well I am a girl, that's not a lie, but I don't think it's right to say "just a girl." Why does he get to say anything about me playing? I wasn't allowed to stand up and tell them I didn't want to play on a travel team or ask why girls can't play hockey. I really shouldn't go over and tell Chris to shut up but suddenly I'm sick of staying quiet because it's not my turn. And all the questions I wanted to ask and all the things I wanted to say in the courtroom are screaming in my brain and I have to say something. Now.

I run over to where Chris and Mr. Fraser are standing, ignoring my mother calling me back, and they both kind of jump like I startled them. Good.

"Tina! I'm so glad you came over. I wanted to talk to you," Mr. Fraser says. "I was just talking to your friend Chris, here. He says you played on the same hockey team this year." Friend? Yeah, some friend.

"Yes, we did." I keep my voice polite for now. I glare at Chris, though, and think, *You can't lie this time!*, hard enough that maybe Chris will hear me.

"So I asked Chris how it was having you on his team, and he—"

"You mean because I'm a girl," I say. I meant to ask it as a question, but it comes out angry. I already know that's what he means.

"Tina, let's go to the car," Mom says. She's beside me, but I didn't notice her follow me. She puts her hand on my arm and gives it a little tug, but I don't move.

"No, no, it's quite all right," Mr. Fraser says to Mom, and then he looks at me. "Yes, because you're a girl, Tina. That's the story here; it's interesting because you're doing something for the first time. You're brave, you know, and people want to know about it."

I don't feel brave. I feel angry, like little bits of anger have been piling up inside my head. It started when Mr. Hickman gave Dad back my registration form and a little bit was added every time someone called me Tony or checked me extra hard or made a face and just now a little bit of angry went in when I saw Chris telling Mr. Fraser lies about how I can't play, and I've never let any of it out and there's no more room in my brain for all the angry thoughts and it's all going to blow out.

"Chris Murray is—" A liar, I mean to say, but the words get stuck because my throat is all tight and I'm going to cry angry tears. I bite my teeth hard together to stop the crying. Blink. Blink.

"Yes, a friend, I know," Mr. Fraser says. "Like I was saying, he was telling me about being on your team and how great a player you are. He said you were the fastest skater on the team and that you had one of the hardest shots even though you weren't one of the biggest kids. That's impressive."

What?

I hear Mr. Fraser, but it takes a minute for my brain to understand. Chris said I was good? I look at Chris. He does that half smile again like he did in the courtroom, and this time I'm pretty sure it does mean he's sorry.

"It's true," Chris says to Mr. Fraser, but he's looking at me. "She's as good as any of the boys out there, better than a lot of them. Why shouldn't she play?"

What? It's like the pile of anger in my head stops growing for a minute. It's not gone, but now I have an extra bit of time before I explode.

Voices get louder, coming up behind us, and I turn to look. Windy-hair man—well, Mr. Murray—and wrinkly-suit man come out of the courthouse together. They're talking and waving their hands around, then they laugh and wrinkly-suit man slaps Mr. Murray on the shoulder. "Excuse me," Mr. Fraser says, but he's already walking away. He turns the page on his notebook and reaches out to touch wrinkly-suit man on the arm to get him to stop walking. Mr. Murray stops too, and he looks over at us and waves. He's waving at Chris, not me.

"Thanks?" I say to Chris.

"Whatever," Chris says. His eyes keep shifting from me to his dad. "You can play, so it's good to have you on my team. Doesn't mean we're friends or anything stupid like that." And he runs away toward his dad without looking back. I watch him cross the parking lot and get into a fancy red car.

"Let's go, Tina," Mom says again. I kind of forgot she was there. She keeps her hand on my arm, but not tugging like before, and we walk to our car. It's hot out in the parking lot. J. R. and I climb into the back seat of the car. The seats are burning and the inside of the car is boiling, so we roll the windows all the way down before we shut the doors. Mom sits in the passenger seat, but she keeps the door open. I lean my arms out the window and watch people come out of the courthouse. Lots of people I recognize from the rink, but I don't remember their names. Mr. Fraser tries to catch them as they come out, but he can't get to everyone.

Finally Dad comes outside. Mr. Fraser calls out his name, but Dad just waves at him and walks right over to the car without talking to anyone else. He gets in the driver's seat and rolls down his window before shutting the door. "Well, what a day," he says. Dad meets my eyes in the rear-view mirror and winks. "Let's go home," he says.

No one talks on the drive home. I look out the window, watching the fields and trees and houses flash by. I'm sleepy and my eyelids are heavy and it's hard to keep my eyes open, but I don't want to fall asleep.

At home Mom goes right into the kitchen and I hear banging around. I go upstairs and change out of my respectable clothes into more comfortable T-shirt and shorts. Then I go back downstairs and find J. R. in the living room. I sit on the couch beside him and look at the TV. I'm not even sure what he's watching, but I stare at it. I'm just so tired.

Mom calls us into the kitchen and I sit in my chair. She puts a plate in front of me: chicken casserole, with biscuits and peas and a creamy sauce. But I'm not hungry.

Dad says, "Tina, stop playing with your food and eat it, please." I poke my fork in a piece of chicken and put it in my mouth to make him happy.

"Do we need to go back tomorrow?" J. R. asks. "I mean, you're all done talking, right?"

"Well, I don't know, J. R., I think it's important that you show support for your sister," Dad says.

"I went today. They didn't even care I was there," J. R. says. He crosses his arms.

"I don't want to go either," I whisper.

"What was that, Tina?" Dad says.

I get a guilty sick feeling in my stomach. Now I really don't want to eat the casserole. I shouldn't complain about going. Dad and Mom and Julia and Mr. Houghman did all the work to go to court to let me play. Mr. Houghman even got them to let me play this year in the meantime. I should go. I should want to go. But I'm tired. "I don't want to go either," I say again. Dad hears me this time. He looks at me as he chews. I look at my plate and make myself eat another piece of chicken.

"It may be interesting tomorrow. They are planning on talking to a university professor who will say that girls and boys are physically able to play the same at your age, and then they'll talk to more people who organize the hockey." When he stops talking I look up at him. He's looking at me like he's trying to figure something out. "Tina, this is your fight," he says.

I have to swallow before I say, "I know."

I need to either just agree to go or make him see why I don't want to. I'm about to explain how I'm tired and how I don't want to listen anymore when people say I'm a problem and that it's wrong for girls to do what boys do. I just don't want to hear it.

"Robert," Mom says before I can say anything, "I think Tina has fought her share. She's stood up for her right to play, and she's dealt with the kids at school and the adults around town. She did so well today in court."

I sneak a glance at Dad. He's still watching me. "Your mother is right, Tina; you have done very well so far. I know it hasn't been easy. Your mother and I are very proud of the way you've handled yourself."

I don't mean to cry, but a bit of a tear slips out and I wipe it with my hand before J. R. can see.

My parents look at each other and both nod a little.

"All right," my dad says. "You two can stay home tomorrow. But I want you to stay close to the house so that if something comes up and they want you back in the courthouse I can come find you. Understood?"

J. R. says, "Yes sir," but my throat still feels funny so I just nod. I feel better and I don't have to try too hard to take a big bite of my supper.

"Will you tell me what happens?" I ask.

"Of course," Dad says. "I'll give you a full report."

CHAPTER 28

A Bike Ride
(August 18, 1978)

WHEN I WAKE UP IN THE MORNING I CAN hear Mom and Dad downstairs. I get out of bed and tiptoe to the top of the stairs. Dad is in his suit, standing by the door. "Pamela, I'll go out and start the car," he says, but then he looks up and sees me. "Good morning, sweetheart. How'd you sleep?"

"Good," I say. But I had a nightmare. I was at school and everyone was yelling at me: "Tony!" and "You just want to be a boy!" and "Go back to Toronto!" and lots of stuff I can't remember. And then it was the courthouse instead of the school and Mr. Rose was there with wrinkly-suit man and windy-hair man and they were all yelling at me too. And the judge was there and he said, "Tony, come up to the stand," but I just sat in my seat because my name is Tina not Tony and he got mad and said I couldn't play hockey. Other than that dream, I slept okay.

Mom comes into the hall and looks up. "Good morning, Tina," she says. She's wearing her light blue pant suit with the big pointy collar and sharp creases down the front of the legs.

"Hi," I say. Maybe I should go with them. I'm not dressed and I haven't brushed my teeth or my hair, but if I hurry....

But then Dad says, "Are you ready, Pamela?" and Mom waves at me and says she's ready and Dad waves at me and says, "Be good. I'll tell you all about it when we get home." And they're gone before I can decide if I want to change my mind or not.

I can hear the car start and then drive away, the *plick-plick* of the tires rolling over gravel in the driveway. And then it's very, very quiet. I sit still and try to hear something. The fridge is making its regular running noise and I hear two caws from the crows outside. If I sit very still I can imagine everyone has gone and I'm all alone in the whole big world and it wouldn't matter if I could play hockey or not because there'd be no one left to play with. But I know the kids from my team this year are at their own houses, waking up or eating breakfast or riding their bikes. And the courthouse probably has a few people in it already, like maybe Julia and Mr. Houghman. Soon Mom and Dad will be there, and the people who need to tell their perspective today, and the judge, who gets to decide if I can play hockey this year or not.

I might as well get on with the day.

I get dressed and brush my hair. In the kitchen, I pour some Fruit Brute cereal in a bowl and drown it with milk. I sit at the table and put the box in front of my bowl to read. The cartoon werewolf looks more like a friendly dog than a monster. I poke the pieces around until I have all pink pieces on my spoon, then all cream ones. I'll eat the marshmallows last. This cereal is really sugary and only for Saturdays. Mom probably wouldn't like me eating it on a weekday, but I'm celebrating the last day at court and that I'm not there. I fill my bowl up with more so I don't waste the milk.

After my cereal I need to make sure to brush my teeth the whole time I'm supposed to. I look in the mirror and try to sing the ABC song in my head, but instead I just keep wondering if the professor will say why people think girls can't play. I'm smaller than some of the boys, but not all of them. I'm faster than a lot of them. I can do all the drills and tricks and moves they can. I wonder about this for probably longer than the ABC song, so I spit out the toothpaste and rinse off my toothbrush. I go down and watch some television. There are no cartoons on because it's not Saturday, I guess. I stand at the TV and turn the knob through the channels, but it's all just adults talking. The commercials are more interesting than any of the shows.

After watching for too long, I go out and shoot on the net. If I do get to play this season, I want to make sure I'm one of the best shooters on my team. I don't want wrinkly-suit man or windy-hair man to have any reason to stop me from playing if the judge says I can. I swing extra hard at the ball and it goes wide, bounces across the gravel, and disappears into the long grass. That was my last ball.

My stomach growls, which is weird since I had two bowls of cereal. But my watch says it's 12:49, which is after lunch, so I guess it makes sense. I head inside. J. R. is sitting in the living room. "What are you watching?" I ask.

He doesn't look up, just says, "*Hogan's Heroes*. Rerun."

"Want a sandwich?" I ask.

He looks at me. "Sure." But he doesn't move.

I make two peanut butter and jelly sandwiches. I put them on plates and bring it out to the living room, even though we're not really supposed to eat in there, and we sit on the couch and eat. The show ends then and another starts with dramatic intro music. It's a dumb soap opera.

I should go for a bike ride. "I'm going to go to the courthouse," I say suddenly.

"What?" J. R. asks. He's looking at me like I have four heads.

But it's really no big deal. "I'm going for a bike ride. I might as well go see what's going on."

"You can't go that far on your own," J. R. says.

I'm not supposed to, but I know the way.

"It's not that far." I try to sound more sure than I am. I probably shouldn't go. Well, I definitely shouldn't go. Biking all the way there would make Mom more mad than eating Fruit Brutes on a weekday. But I'm going.

"Tina, you're not allowed to go alone!" J. R. says. I already know that, but he can't tell me what to do. Or what not to do.

"You're not the boss of me!" I shout and run out of the house.

My bike is leaning against his, and when I try to pull mine up, the handlebars and one of the pedals are tangled in his bike. I pull on mine, then push on his to get them apart, but they're stuck. I stand between them and try to turn the pedal enough to get it loose, but the front tire turns out and the whole bike slides down so the handlebars are pushed even farther into J. R.'s.

I stand up a minute. My eyes are prickly and I squeeze them shut. Count to ten: one, two, three, four...I hear J. R.'s feet on the steps. If he's out here to tell me what I'm not allowed to do, I'm going to punch him, I swear. I don't care if I get in more trouble.

I open my eyes and he's standing in front of me. He's wearing a sweater and holding out my blue Sabres sweatshirt. "It's cool today. You're going to get cold," he says. I take the sweatshirt and put it on and J. R. wiggles the bikes apart. "Let's go," he says, getting on his bike and coasting down the driveway. I hop on mine and follow.

It doesn't take us too long to bike into town. Maybe a half hour later, I follow J. R. into the courthouse parking lot. Dad's car is parked in the same place as yesterday. J. R. and I pull our bikes up the steps and lean them against the wall on one side of the entrance, out of the way. He pulls the heavy door open and holds it for me to walk in first. I can't believe how nice he's being.

Inside it's cool. Even though it's not very hot outside and I'm glad I have my sweatshirt on, the bike ride made me sweaty on my neck. The sweat gets cold in the courthouse and I shrug my shoulders, trying to dry my neck on the back of my shirt. We walk over to the courtroom, but when J. R. puts his hand on the handle to pull it open, a man comes up to him and puts his hand on his shoulder.

"You can't go in there, son; there's a meeting in progress," he says.

"I know," J. R. says, "but she's Tina Forbes."

"I don't care if she's Santa Claus, you children can't go in there right now," the man says.

"But it's her case!" J. R. says. "She had to talk on the stand yesterday and everything. She's only eleven, come on."

The man takes his hand off J. R. and I think he's going to let us in. But he doesn't. He crosses his arms and glares at us. He doesn't say anything, but I think he's thinking, "Go ahead and try it." We don't try it. Finally he says, "You can sit there and wait, if you want."

J. R. and I walk over to the bench across the hall from the door and the uniformed man walks back and sits behind a desk and picks up a book. "I guess we'll just wait for Mom and Dad here. Are you okay?" J. R. says as he sits down.

Has he ever asked me this before? Has an alien abducted my brother and left me with someone... nice? "I'm okay. Why did you come with me?" Honestly, I'm just hoping to hear some more nice things from him.

"Mom and Dad would've killed me if I hadn't." He glances at me, then looks back at his shoes. "Anyway, I get why you want to come. Maybe this is a big deal. Maybe if you weren't so annoying, I might be a little proud of you."

I can't believe it. I start to say something, but he glares at me. "Don't get all mushy. Ugh." He crosses his arms and glares at the guard.

I feel a little glow in my chest. I don't think J. R. has ever even not been cranky with me before, let alone actually proud of me. But I keep quiet and try to entertain myself so I don't break the spell.

Sitting on this bench, J. R.'s feet reach to the floor. Mine hang in the air and I can't help but swing them back and forth, touching the toe of my sneaker on the floor as it goes by. It makes a *squeak, squeak, squeak* sound. The man keeps looking up and staring at me, but I don't stop. Beside me J. R. snickers and I squeak the next one extra loud.

I'm trying to get my eyes to follow the ceiling fan fast enough to see the blade turning instead of the blurred circle when the door bangs open. I jump and J. R. laughs at me. We wait until the first bunch of people have come out, but Mom and Dad aren't there, so we go inside. Mom and Dad are standing at the front of the courtroom with Julia and Mr. Houghman.

Mom sees us when we're walking up and says, "J. R.! Tina! How did you get here?"

"We biked," I say. I look closely at her eyes to see if she's going to get mad about that. She looks serious for a minute, then smiles. Phew.

"We didn't get here in time, though," J. R. says. "The guard wouldn't let us in. He made us wait in the hall so we didn't hear anything they said."

"What did everyone say? Did the doctor say girls can play sports just like boys?" I have a million questions all of a sudden.

Dad puts his arm around J. R.'s shoulders and pats my head. "How about we give you all the details on our way home?"

"Is it over?" I ask.

Julia nods and says, "It went well, Tina. I think we made a good case, and your testimony was very helpful." She's smiling at me.

"When will we know?" That's probably the most important question right now.

Mr. Houghman says, "Judge Kimberly said he wants it finished before registration. He will write up his decision and we'll know before the end of September."

My stomach buzzes a bit. It feels like a long time to wait to hear. "Okay," I say because everyone is looking at me and waiting for me to say something.

"Shall we go home?" Dad says, and Mom agrees. Dad slips his hand around mine. I'm too old to hold hands, but his is warm and tight as we walk out. When we get outside, J. R. and I bring our bikes down the stairs, the back wheels bouncing off each step. Dad wiggles them into the back of the car. The hatch won't close, but that doesn't matter. We don't have far to go.

I slide into the seat behind Dad's and roll down the window. I can smell the grass and the salt water in the air. Soon it'll smell more like fall: leaves and campfires, reminding me of school and Halloween and apples and hockey.

CHAPTER 29

A New First Day
(September 1978)

SOME KIDS GET BORED AT THE END OF SUMMER break and can't wait to go back to school. I don't get it. I could never get tired of baseball and golf and tennis and bike riding and shooting hoops and pucks. I'd rather do all of those than go to school. Still, the first day of school arrives. I'm wearing my new *Muppet Show* T-shirt with Animal sitting by his drums. He's my favourite.

Shari is waiting for me when I stop to get her. She comes running out of her house and meets me on the sidewalk. She's wearing a new dress and shiny black shoes. She won't want to play ball at recess then, that's for sure.

When we reach school there are already lots of kids in the yard. It's strange how everything is the same but also feels a little bit different. Since I'm a bit bigger, there are fewer kids who are bigger than me and more who are smaller, and the primary kids look really tiny, even tinier than last year.

Shari points toward the doors. "Look, there's Lindsay and Michelle! Come on! I want to hear about Michelle's trip to Toronto this summer." Shari grabs my arm and I let her pull me over to the group of girls standing in a group by the door. I stand with them, but I don't pay attention. I'm watching the boys running back and forth on the grass. One group has a soccer ball and one group is throwing a football. It's hard to tell who's in which group, they're just running and laughing. Near us is another group of girls whispering and laughing. I'd rather be on the grass.

"I'm going to go—" But the bell rings before I can say "play ball." We line up in our new classes, and when the teacher points to my line, we walk into the school.

THE TEACHER GAVE US HOMEWORK on the first day! Grade five is going to be tough. We had to find a book in the library when we went this afternoon, and now we have to look at the cover and read the part on the back that's called a "summary" and we have to finish a worksheet and answer some questions about the book based on what we can tell from the cover. I picked *Tales of a Fourth Grade Nothing* by Judy Blume and I've already answered all the questions. The last thing I have to do is read the first chapter, and I want to get that done so I have time to go out and shoot at the net. Hockey season is coming up and I need to be ready. I hope.

I put my bookmark at the end of chapter one so I can see how far I have to go and start on the first page. I've read three pages when I hear Dad's car come up the driveway. He's home early. I move the bookmark to save my spot and toss the book on the bed behind me as I race out of my room to say hello. I won't ask about the court decision. Four days ago when I asked, he said, "Tina, you don't have to ask every day. I'll be sure to let you know." It was hard to tell if he was joking or really kind of mad, so I decided not to ask anymore.

I fly down the stairs two at a time. Dad's by the door taking off his shoes and putting on his slippers.

"Hi, Dad," I say. I hope it doesn't sound like I want to ask about the decision.

"Hi, Tina Marie. How was your day?"

"Good. We got homework already."

"You did? What do you have to do?"

I shrug and say, "Read a book," which is true.

"A whole book?" he says, making a ridiculous surprised face. I laugh.

I follow him into the kitchen, where Mom is cooking supper. "Hello, Rob, you're home early," she says.

"I am," Dad says, but he's smiling at me, not Mom. "I have news."

News. He's smiling at me. It must be the court decision. What else could it be? My throat is too tight to say anything and my chest is burning. I'm holding my breath. I make myself take a big breath in, like Julia taught me when we were practicing the questions. My stomach is jumpy. I'm staring at Dad, but even though I don't think he'd mind if I asked, I can't say anything at all.

Luckily, Mom says, "What is it, Rob? Did you hear from the judge?"

Dad nods. He flicks the latches on his briefcase and the cover pops open. His briefcase is always full of papers. He lifts some off the top and holds it up for Mom and me to see. There are words in a title down the middle of the page and I see my name about halfway down. Dad hands it to me. There must be a thousand pages to it. It's thicker than *Tales of a Fourth Grade Nothing*. I flip to the end and the last page has the number twenty-seven on it. Okay, so not quite a thousand. But a lot.

"What does it say?" I ask. My voice sounds funny, like I have a cold.

Dad holds his hand out and I give it back to him. He flips through to one of the last pages and starts to read: "In my opinion the complainant is entitled to be registered in the Yarmouth Minor Hockey Association and she is entitled to play hockey in competition over which the YMHA has control and direction. Pursuant to Section 26A (8) of the Human Rights Act, I order that the YMHA process the application for registration of the complainant Tina Marie Forbes in the same manner that any other application for registration in the YMHA is processed."

When he stops, I can't stop staring at him. "Do you know what that means, Tina?"

I do, but I'm scared to believe it. I keep staring.

"It means you did it," Mom says. "You did it, Tina. You won. You fought to play hockey and you stood up against discrimination and you won! You get to play!"

"I do?" I ask, even though I heard just fine.

"You do," Dad says. Then they're both hugging me. And I can't stop smiling. I'm smiling so much my cheeks hurt.

When they let go of me I say, "I'm going outside."

"What for?" Dad asks.

"I have to go take some shots," I say. "I have to get ready for the season."

Afterword

THIS BOOK IS BASED ON THE TRUE STORY OF Tena Forbes, who really did fight to play hockey in Yarmouth in the 1970s. And she really did win! This isn't her exact story—it's fictionalized, so most of the dialogue is made up—but because court proceedings are recorded, I was able to use very closely (and in some cases word for word) what everyone said on the stand. Tena finished high school in Yarmouth and played minor hockey until she was fifteen.

Today she lives in Ontario, where she works for Toyota checking the quality of parts during car assembly. In her free time Tena still loves all sorts of sports, including skiing, swimming, hiking, dirt biking, and skating in her "Vapes" (Bauer Vapor skates). She loves the roller coasters at Wonderland.

Tena now has two adult sons who also love sports. She visits Nova Scotia regularly and is still friends with Shari. While the Buffalo Sabres were her favourite when she was young, these days she cheers loudest for the Vancouver Canucks.

Acknowledgements

"Women's sport helps break down a lot of barriers for women in other areas, whether in religion or politics."

–Clare Balding

This book is fictional; the characters were figments of my imagination. However, this novel was inspired by a true story, a real person and her very real determination to work towards the right to participate. I am so thankful to Tena Forbes for sharing her story with me and allowing me the freedom to create characters that bring her lessons to readers.

*"A good coach can change a game,
a great coach can change a life."*

–John Wooden

Organized sports were a huge contribution to my growing up, and continue to be an important part of my children's lives. You'll find me sitting by the pools, gyms, fields, courts, barns, and rinks watching them find themselves. The volunteer coaches who show up to these sports are essential. My girls were fortunate to have a great coach, Jim Rossiter, who knew just how to use sport to grow their hockey development, their leadership skills, their personal confidence and values, their team play and friendship. He told them Tena's story as an example of determination and effort and I was lucky enough to be in the dressing room to hear it. Jim's daughter, Kate, is a fantastic hockey player and an exceptional first reader who gave me invaluable feedback on early drafts.

"All kids need is a little help, a little hope and someone who believes in them."
                                    –Magic Johnson

My love for sport was nurtured by my parents' efforts to bring me to all the pools, gyms, fields, courts, barns, and rinks…. They came as my cheerleaders then and continue to be my biggest source of support.

Acknowledgements

"Never let the fear of striking out keep you from playing the game."

–Babe Ruth

Finally my favourite athletes, Jack, Elliot, Paxten, and AnnaWen, show me over and over why it's important to get back up, shake off the sting, and get back in the game. I've all but given up on an NHL career for them to support me in old age, but they are fantastic people who bring their sport skills into life.

Other Books By Natalie Corbett Sampson

Aptitude

Set in a dystopian future where everyone has a role and no one is given a choice in their life's path, *Aptitude* is the story of a young woman's struggle to decide between two men: the one society chose for her, and the one she's fallen in love with.

It Should Have Been a #GoodDay

Ella must navigate more than most kids her age: tough decisions with even tougher consequences. Could her challenges be Katherine's solution, or will they just lead to more heartache?

Game Plan

Going about the trials of everyday life, no one knows how their path might cross another's...and change them both forever.

Take These Broken Wings

Layne Wheeler loves lists. Lists put her life in order and lists to help plan when things go off the rails. Stepping on a skateboard to impress her crush wasn't on any of Layne's lists. Her accident triggers a cascade of events that spins her life so out of control no list can fix it.